I0538104

Synopsis

Kristen is a hot headed beauty that loves playing hard to get. Her mother compels her to marry the handsome and seductive Drake Montreal. Kristen is forced to go on a vacation to a secluded island to see if marriage is feasible. Kristen's mother has a vision of personal gain. Drake wants to keep playing the field but is more than willing to accept the challenge of the beautiful young Kristen Whitmore. Kristen wants no part in an arranged marriage, but their Hearts will decide if it's for love or money.

.

For Love or Money

Freda Roberts

Chapter 1

"So what's been up with your mom lately?" my friend Lisa asked as she looked at me over her sunglasses. We were in our favorite spot, where the sun hits the best on this shadowed beach. We were catching up on our tan, because if the truth was told, I was pale as could be.

I laughed, "I don't know, maybe she's finally going to tie the knot, right?" I laughed at the thought. "Who knows why she has been to thousands of bridal shops Lisa, maybe, just maybe, she likes the dresses," I said.

She laughed, "My ass, she likes those dresses, I'm still suspicious." I rolled my eyes at her. She was always being paranoid.

"I think I'm done," I said as I stood up and looked at my almost red arms.

"See, this is why you can't get a decent tan, you don't take the time to fully enjoy the sun." She said shaking her head.

"Yea but still, I don't want to end up look like a baked potato." I said.

She laughed. "Are you going to stay," I asked.

"Yea, just for a while." she answered.

"Alright then, have it your way." I went to get my towel and beach bag, and started walking.

"Nice ass!" she screamed laughing. I rolled my eyes and laughed. She can be so immature sometimes.

As I entered our beach house I heard my mom screaming at the chefs for making her toast too soft. She could really over exaggerate things sometimes. I was so tired, all I wanted to do was lie down in my bed, and stay there for the next week. Just to think of going up stairs was pure agony for my legs. I proceeded to my room, and as I opened my bedroom door I nearly fainted, not from fatigue, but out of absolute shock. Spread across my bed was the most beautiful white dress. At first I thought it was just a normal dress for some formal party or something. But as I got closer, and let me tell you, it took me a long time, I saw the beautiful curves and detail; all I could do was scream "MOM!"

She came in and stopped in the doorway, she looked amused, damn her.

"Yes, honey?" She acted all sweet like. I pointed at the dress spread freely on my bed.

She sighed, "Well what do you think it is? It's a wedding dress of course." She said it like it was the most causal thing in the world.

"I know what it is. I was just wondering what it is doing on my bed." Keep it calm Kristen, keep calm.

My mom laughed. "Kristen, honey, you're going to be engaged." All I could do was stare at her, what did she mean by I'm going to be engaged?

"What do you mean by en-engaged?" I choked on the words.

"Well you're going to be married Kristen, its simple."

"Mother, we're talking about marriage, and at the age of 19, this is anything but simple," I said through gritted teeth. "I don't even know the guy!" I glared at her in anger," Or woman? Holy shit, what has she mom gotten me into?

"It's a man, honey, flesh and blood." Relief shot through me, but not all of it. I hear footsteps coming up the stairs, Lisa enters the room. She looked wide eyed at the dress and looked from me to the dress non-stop. "You've got to be screwing with me right?" She laughed so hard she literally falls to all fours. I stared at her, she was supposed to be my best friend and this is all she does in a situation like this.

"Oh Lisa, shut the hell up, this is not funny alright!" She stood up straightening her bikini top; she wiped tears from her eyes. "It's from my point of view!"

"So who's the lucky guy," Lisa asked, as she gained control of her laughter. "Ask her," I pointed to my mom. My mom stood by my bed looking at me, "I'm not telling until you two ask politely."

"Mom do you realize how stupid you sound right now, you engaged me, and I want to know who he is right now!" Lisa nodded in agreement behind me to make it final.

"Fine," she gave up. I glared at her, I saw Lisa looking at my mother in anticipation, like a child who ate all her broccoli and was now getting a big sweet treat.

"So who is he?" I said.

"Drake Montréal," she said. I stared at her wide eyed. I saw Lisa's mouth literally drop down to the floor.

Chapter 2

"Lucky bastard," Sandra yelled over the music I had booming in my room. I lay face down in my bed, trying to drain out all the horrifying thoughts of being engaged. My days of being a bachelorette are over. Damn my mother, and her damn plans. Sandra turned off the music, while I groaned in response. I raised my face an inch. "I'm everything but lucky, don't you get it. Who in the hell told you to turn the music off, turn it back on."

"Oh shut up, little Ms. Grumpy. I'm not turning the music back on. You're lucky, believe me. I have a hard time telling myself not to kill you and posing myself as your clone." She said with a smile. I threw my pillow at her, I guess I was pretty mad because the next thing I saw Sandra on the floor looking surprised.

"Holy Shit Sandra, I'm sorry!" I got off the bed and pulled her to her feet. She eyed me with that 'I can't believe you just did that' kind of glare.

"I'm trying to be nice, and all I get is a freaking concussion?" She put her hands up to her hips.

I laughed, "First of all, I highly doubt you have a concussion, and second, I said I was sorry, that should be enough for you."

"Well it's not," she looked at me with an amused smile, "but this will,"

I looked at her in confusion. "Get down on your knees and beg, until I forgive you." I laughed so hard I snorted.

"Easy Hitler, I don't want any problems," I raised my hands in surrender.

"Okay, okay, if you insist, I forgive you," She said while rolling her eyes.

"Anyways back to the whole Drake--"

"Drake is so handsome!" She cut me off. "Open your eyes Kristen, have you seen those muscles, those abs, and those eyes. Holy shit! Those eyes Kristen, you know I'm a sucker for green eyes and--"

"Alright, my god I think I get it!" I said a little too loud for my own liking. She looked at me as if I just threw her some cold water.

"You don't get it, Kristen; stop lying to yourself" she laughed.

I felt my face grow hot. Maybe Drake Montréal was hot in every way; he might have a great body, great eyes, and all. But he wasn't my type, at all. I was going to reply to Sandra's comment but we were disturbed by the knocking of the door.

"Kristen, honey, may I come in," mom asked. Why does she have to ask, she already took my freedom away. She was the queen of this house why not come tumbling in.

"No!" I yelled before I had time to think what I was saying.

She wasn't going to come in, not in a million years, over my dead body. She came in anyways. Great, what I said did nothing.

"Get your stuff ready, we're leaving." She threw me my suitcase, and started looking into my drawers.

"I'm not going anywhere, and what makes you think you can look through my drawers; my personal things."

"Well I can think of two reasons: one, I'm your mother, second: your fiancé's waiting." She looked at me proud of her reasons. I glared at her, not only because she was right, but because she left me without anything to say. Sandra stayed quiet in the corner, so much for being my best friend.

"Fine," That was all I could say. Lame right, yeah well, tell me about it.

"Oh can I come?" Sandra raised her hand excitingly.

"No," I said firmly

"Why the hell not, I want to see your fiancé?" She bit her lip seductively causing me to roll my eyes, "I said, Fine."

She clapped her hands and started jumping up and down in anticipation, "Well first I have to get rid of this bikini and put something at least slightly skimpy," she said to herself. Sandra continued, "Oh my god! I need to shave these legs," she bent down and eyed her thighs closely. I laughed.

"I thought you were going to say you needed a bikini wax,"

"Ha-ha, you're so damn funny," and with that she disappeared into the bathroom. I saw my mom in the doorway, looking at me with concern. I glared at her as I turned around and shoved one of my shirts hard into my bag.

"Sweetie, are you alright?"

I laughed harshly

"Oh yea mom, I'm super duper right now, hence me shoving my things into my bag! Of course I'm not alright, you just engaged me to someone I barely even know, and aside from all that you still have the nerve to ask me if I'm alright!" I couldn't give a rats-ass that I was shouting at my own mother, she deserved it! I dropped on my knees and began to cry.

"How could you do this to me?" I sobbed.

"I'm sorry," I heard her say, soon followed by the stomping of her feet down the stairs. I wiped the salty tears away from my eyes with the brim of my shirt. Keep it strong Kristen; just keep it strong, I thought. After I finished packing my stuff, I saw Sandra coming out of the shower, with her skin glowing.

She was wearing a short denim skirt, and when I say short, I mean a short denim skirt with a light purple tank top that showed off perfect curves and just below her belly button so you can see her belly piercing. "I remember when you got that," I said pointing at her piercing.

She shivered at the memory. "Yes, don't remind me. My parents popped like 15 veins," I laughed and nodded my head in disagreement, "Don't exaggerate."

"Yeah, you're right," she said. "They only popped 13, thanks for reminding me," she smiled. She sat next to me on my bed and wrapped her arms around my shoulders, "Everything is going to be okay Kristen, don't worry about it."

I sighed, "Easy for you to say."

Twenty minutes later we went down to the car. Daniel, the chauffer put our bags into the back of the car. My mom got in without glancing back.

Sandra was trying hard not to show her Victoria's Secret underwear while getting into the car which wasn't possible because her skirt kept shooting up. I had the urge to laugh. Sandra was beautiful, she had long strawberry blond hair that curled at the tips, and she had wonderful curves that any girl would kill for. Yeah, she might be wild and crazy sometimes, but hey, that was Sandra, life and soul of the party.

Me, well I have brunette color hair that fell under my shoulders, a decent body with decent curves, a few freckles on my nose, and hazel eyes. My eyes were nothing compared to Sandra's who's were Caribbean blue and were highlighted by long eyelashes. I envied her.

I sighed, the car was beginning to move, and I was going to miss it here. Good-bye Florida, my sunshine state. Sandra grabbed my hand and patted it, "its okay, Kris," she told me, "And besides if he ends up being an asshole, I still have my grizzly handcuffs and a pair of scissors." She winked at me.

I laughed at her words. Did I fail to mention Sandra was a bit on the crazy side?

Chapter 3

We were well into the third hour of driving, Sandra and I made occasional conversations that excluded my mother. I was staring out the window when it hit me.

"Mom, why do I need my suitcase?" My heart quickened, please God, don't let it be what I think it is.

"Didn't I tell you?"

"Tell me what," I looked at Sandra expecting that she had an answer, she just shrugged but looked worried, I guess it was my facial expressions reflected onto hers.

"Well," my mom hesitated.

"Well," I pressed on,

"You and Drake are going on vacation, me and Peter; you know his dad, planned it all," she said," since you don't know anything about Drake."

"Yea I actually do know a thing or two about Drake, he's cocky and overly flirtatious, there, that's all I need to know." I said firmly crossing my arms in my chest, how can't I know. I mean his dad was a millionaire; Drake had the looks and the money, which is what most girls aim for in a man. Plus, pictures don't lie, and let me tell you, the paparazzi do take convincing pictures. My mom turned around from her seat and stared at me.

"Kristen what's wrong with a man having confidence?" Oh dear mother, I have the perfect answer to that.

"Mom there's having confidence and there's having too much confidence, learn to distinguish the two." There now turn around and leave me alone. "Yup, that's kind of true Ms. Whitmore," Sandra said, finally she backed me up.

"Thank you Sandra, now will you please tell me what you people planned," I said, I wasn't going to let it go. Not until I had an answer.

"You and Drake are going on vacation to one of his Father's private island," Sandra stayed quiet next to me, and as for me, I exploded.

"You what," I screamed, "Its one thing to marry me off to some jackass, but now I have to go on vacation with him to some island, just to make it official!"

Sandra patted me on the shoulder, but I flipped her off, she didn't expect me to keep calm in a situation like this did she? I was shaking with anger, and sure enough close to tears. My mom was staring at me from the passenger seat, "Kristen, calm down," shock drained her face replaced by calmness. I sighed, "I'm sorry, it's just that," I rubbed my forehead; a tear escaped my eyes without my permission, so much for staying strong. "Never mind," I said.

I bent down to get my I-pod from my bag, but came across something entirely different. I grabbed a small package, and held it up to my face. Aw fuck condoms.

I felt my face turn beet red, I heard Sandra laugh next to me, I turned around, and her face was almost purple from laughter. "Mom would you care to explain why the hell there's condoms inside my bag!" I watched Daniel blush at the sight, wonder what that meant? Her phone rang; she searched through her big-ass Prada handbag.

"Well honey, I thought you might need them, you know just in case, always be prepared." What kind of mother would hand her daughter condoms.

Sandra was enjoying this, "Look!" she screamed, "There's more, lubricant. Non-lubricant, flavored, wow Ms. Whitmore you go all out!" She laughed harder. I searched through my bag nervously making sure what she said wasn't true, sure enough she wasn't lying.

"Mom, seriously, I'm not a teenager who's desperate for sex!" I said grabbing the pile from Sandra's hands and shoved them deep into my bag, my God she looked at them as if they were made out of gold.

"You never know honey," she smiled as if nothing happened. "Oh and that was Peter, Kristen fix that birds nest of your, we're almost there." She said soon followed by silence.

I took the silence in advantage and asked," Mom, why exactly do I have to marry Drake?" She took a while to answer which meant two things: either she was thinking of a good lie to tell me or she was actually thinking of how to best put it.

"Well remember I told you I was having problems with my business," I nodded, "Well we lost money Kristen, and this is by far the best way to recover it."

"So you're using me as your own personal bank? Way to go mom, you just lost your only ticket out of a nursing home," I said, I knew my mom shivered at the thought of having to go a nursing home, so Ha! That's exactly the place you're going for putting me through this hell.

"Try looking at this situation from my point of view, honey." She said with a worried look in her eyes.

"Whatever mom," She sighed and didn't disturb me any longer.

I looked around the window for a distraction, the house around this neighborhood were luxurious and extremely big. Yea we had money, quite a large amount actually, but I was guessing not like these people. The houses were like castles, not exaggerating, they had beautiful details and perfect cut grass. Each house we passed bigger than the last, hard to believe right. But true.

"We're here!" My mom screamed suddenly, I thought we were never getting out of that stupid car. I turned around, I could feel my eyes go wide, and this house right in front of me had to be the best in this whole neighborhood. Brazilian Cherry doors detailed by golden outlines, even the driveway looked expensive. Don't even get me started on the cars, Lamborghinis and Ferraris covered the whole place. To summarize it all the house looked like a fairy tale castle and the richest one at that. Sandra gasped, her mouth forming a small O.

"Well, should we go in or what?" My mom broke the silence.

"Uh-huh," Sandra said as she got out of the car. It took us well enough five minutes to get to the doors. Do they always have to walk that long-ass driveway or do they have golf carts?

When we finally got to the door my mom rang the bell. A man opened the door, his face with no expression, around his late forties to early fifties. He was about to say something but got interrupted by a low husky voice. "Now, now Freddy why don't you let our lovely guests come in, they might be freezing." I knew sure as hell I was.

"I n-know I-I am," Sandra said through cluttering teeth. I snorted, poor her. She rolled her eyes at me; she knew what I was thinking alright.

"This way ladies" Freddy bowed and started walking. We followed, I stared at the living room in awe, it might have been simple with light blue walls, some family photos here and there, but the simplicity of it all made it look even more beautiful.

"Hello Eliza, beautiful as ever," A man, that I must say was way too handsome for someone his age, grabbed my mom's hand and kissed it formally. He had sleek black hair that reached under his ears, grey eyes that twinkled, and even though he might be in his early forties you can clearly tell that under his suit there was a healthy looking body, I wouldn't be surprised if you found a 6-pack under there.

"Oh Peter you know exactly what to say to make me blush," My mom said giggling; Peter laughed and turned his attention to me.

"And you must be Kristen, or am I mistaken?" He said pointing a long finger at me, I smiled politely and said, "Yep, the one and only."

"Well it's very nice to finally meet you; your mother has told me so much about you." I turned to my mom; I gritted my teeth and smiled.

"Oh, has she now?" I asked.

"Quite frankly," as he smiled and exposed those pearly whites, he looked over at Sandra and said, "And you are?" he asked politely

"I'm Sandra, Kristen's best friend, nice to meet you sir," she stuck her hand out, he shook it and kissed it as well, Sandra smiled.

"So Peter where is Drake," my mom asked while looking around,
"He's in his bedroom, I'm sure he'll be down here soon, care to have seat?" He pointed at some lovely looking couches. I sat down without hesitation, my legs were killing me! Sandra glared at the couches, I gave her my sweater so she can cover he exposed legs. "Thanks," she whispered.

"So Eliza how have you been" Peter asked?

"Fine, we just came back from the beach house in Florida."

"I forgot you had house over there," He asked rubbing his chin.

"We haven't been there in years,"

"That would explain it." He laughed. They kept laughing and talking like old friends.

A while later I heard footsteps coming from the marble staircase, I turned around to find myself being locked into a gaze with the most beautiful green eyes I have ever seen in my nineteen years of existence. I scattered my eyes to the rest of his body, Sandra wasn't exaggerating when she said Drake had an amazing body, because he did and amazingly a gorgeous looking tan. He was wearing faded blue jeans with a white tee shirt, even when he wasn't trying he looked overwhelmingly sexy. He had full irresistible lips, and dark brown hair. This time I knew I was the one whose mouth literally fell to the floor.

Chapter 4

"Umm...Hello," the Greek God in front of me said. His voice was low and surprisingly sexy, and apparently he didn't know who we were.

"Ah, Drake, come here," his dad stood up and motioned his hand to come closer. Drake hesitated for a moment but quickly moved closer. A smile was slowly creeping to the corners of his mouth. Holy Shit! Oh my God, Kristen keep it together, this guy right in front of you is the whole reason you're in this mess, remember! But I couldn't help but stare. One thing is for sure, he looked way better in person. He came to halt next to his father and stared at me. His smile reached its peak; I found it very annoying for some reason, like he knew he was better than me. I wasn't going to be easy with him.

"Drake this is Kristen Whitmore, your fiancée," Peter said grinning nervously. Drake smirked at this while I just glared at him with hatred.

"Nice to meet you, Kristen," he smiled. Bull-shit, I sang in my head. I could tell he hated me on the inside, because I'm the reason he can't party till 6 and have sex with every girl he wants, too bad for him.

"Likewise," was the only thing I said? It wasn't nice to meet him, quite the opposite actually. Peter went on, feeling the tension growing between me and my fiancé.

"This is her lovely mother, Eliza, and this is her best friend," Drake shook Sandra's hand.

"Nice to meet you Sandra," he said with a smile,

"Oh the pleasure is all mine," Sandra said sensually.

I laughed loudly. She was beginning to flirt with him and this early, Sandra and her hormones. Everyone stared at me, "I just remembered a funny joke," I lied.

"Well Drake why don't you show Kristen around?" Peter suggested, I felt myself going rigid, they were doing this on purpose, Screw them!

"Okay," he shrugged, "this way Kristen," he showed me the way up the stairs. I followed slowly, too tense to keep up with him. I glanced at my mom and Sandra, my mother was smiling with satisfaction and Sandra looked like she wanted to strangle me, but smiled. She was jealous; I was so going to tease her about this.

We reached the top of the stairs, and I wasn't surprised when I saw a maze of bedrooms before my eyes.

"So Kristen..." he said showing me another room.

"Don't talk to me." I grumbled. He chuckled,

"Well you are going to be my fiancé," he said as he leaned in closer. I scooted away,

"Don't flatter yourself. I'm not like every other girl you see. I'm not easy, so I suggest you back the hell up." I finished.

"Oh I didn't plan on you being easy," he leaned in closer.

"You're invading my space," I pushed him away.

"You mean our space," he laughed, "What's mine is yours, and vice versa, remember."

He tapped my head gently, while I flinched away. He laughed as my eyes turned to slits, what the hell did he find so funny?

I sighed madly and told him, "Where's my bedroom?"

He pointed to a bedroom right across the hall, it looked big enough. "Thanks," I said coldly, and started to turn around, but a hand grabbed me by my wrist. I felt a sensation go down my body, I ignored it. I turned around to see a pair of green eyes.

"Goodnight Kristen, I'm looking forward to our vacation." He winked at me and started to walk away. Shit, I thought, I forgot about that.

Drake's POV:

As I started to walk away, I turned my head slightly. Kristen was already gliding towards her room. Wow, that was a sight to see.

I'm not easy. Her voice rang in my head. That was different, I was used to girls swarming all over me, but for some reason Kristen wasn't. Am I losing my powers of persuasion? No, that can't be it; her friend seemed stunned and flirty enough. It did feel good though, refreshing you may call it.

Kristen was a beauty. She had an awesome body and she held her head up high with dignity. Those cute freckles on her nose, the rosy cheeks and hazel eyes could knock any guy out of his socks. We were going to get married a week or two after returning from vacation, nothing big, but just to make it official. I mean don't get me wrong, Kristen was hot but this isn't the way I play. I have not taken the time to really get to know any girl, talking, and then maybe a little time to satisfy my needs while planning to just let her down easy, trying not to make a big deal out of it is just not my style. I have never lasted a good month with any girl, not because I'm a player, but just because they're not what I'm looking for. But hey, if we're going to get divorced in a month or two after this small wedding, then why not have a little fun. I smiled to myself; I might just have a little fun.

Kristen's POV:

I sat on the bed inside this big room. This room was too luxurious to be a guest room. But hey with everything else in this house it seemed perfectly normal.

"Knock, Knock, said the big bad wolf," Sandra laid herself next to me and turned around on her side to look at me more closely. I noticed she changed into more comfortable looking clothes; skinny jeans and her favorite orange Hollister shirt.

"I noticed how you looked at my fiancé, you slut." I put my hands on my hips and looked at her with fake anger. I ended up giggling; I couldn't put a mad face on with her without laughing my ass off. She giggled too, and put her hand to her forehead as if she was going to faint.

"Well my darling, you don't want him, why not take him while I have the chance," I turned at Sandra and narrowed my eyes.

"What's that suppose to mean?" I asked her.

"Oh c'mon Kristen, you can't be that ignorant," She looked at me, thinking what she just said cleared everything up for me.

"I still don't get you."

"You, Drake and no one else all alone on a deserted island I mean, seriously something is bound to happen, and when it does you won't want to share him."

She can't be serious.

Chapter 5

SPLASH!

I rose from my sleep, gasping and running my hands through my cold wet hair. "What the FUCK!" I yelled gasping for needed oxygen. Oh hell no! Whoever did this going to get their ass peeled, and I was going to enjoy every single minute of it.

"Wake up honey, said my mother" as I rubbed my eyes trying to get water out of them. Damn, I couldn't believe she just did that! I mean, the last time she did this was when I was 10, and she was late to an "important" fashion show.

"Mom, what the HELL is wrong with you?"

"Kristen will you please stop using bad language? I needed to wake you up. I tapped and shoved you for the hundredth time already." She said as she put the bucket aside and sat beside me on the wet bed.

"No! You just splashed me with water! And what's wrong with them, huh? Not like they hurt anybody. Fuck, fuck, fuck, fuck, fuck!" I swung my feet to the side so I could get away from that woman. She sighed, giving up; I went to the bathroom and changed into some sweats and a white tank top. I wasn't in the mood to play dress up. I swung open the door and found Sandra sitting in the non-wet part of my bed, my mother was nowhere in sight. Good! She knew what was best for her.

"I heard you cursing your ass off, bad girl," she rubbed her two index fingers together saying "Shame on you." I gave her the finger; I wasn't in the mood for a chat either. She walked up to me and poked my stomach. "Why are you so grumpy this morning?" I sat next to her; I didn't give a crap I sat in the wet spot.

"You would too if you were woken up with cold water from Antarctica." She looked at me and smiled.

"Harsh," she laughed. "You're such a grump when you're being woken up when you don't want to. Let's face it you would probably hibernate in your damn bed if no one woke you up." I laughed, sort of true. I was a heavy sleeper but that was because I barely had time to sleep, so don't blame me, blame school. I guess it became a habit.

"Why did she wake me up this early anyways?" Sandra looked at me incredulously.

"Are you kidding me, it's 11. Who knows, why you don't ask her."

Maybe she was right. I just got splashed with cold water; of course I needed an explanation. I went down the same staircase as before going as slow a possible thinking I might slip, they looked so polished. I looked around and saw my mom eating her breakfast and talking to Peter. He turned around and smiled a tired smile at me. I smiled back thinking it was the most polite thing to do.

"Good Morning Kristen," He said as he motioned me to a chair in the between him and my mom.

"Did you sleep well? Looks like you took a shower," he said looking at me wet hair.

"I slept well enough, but for some reason I woke up wet this morning." Nice choice of words Kristen, now he's going to think you're a horny little pervert. Good enough for me he didn't notice.

"Oh honey, I'm sorry I went to your bedroom this morning to take you a fresh cup of water and I tripped on my own two feet. I'm sorry." Yea right, my ass you tripped. But I had to just play along.

"Oh, it's okay mom after all it was just an accident," I said bitterly.

"I'm such a klutz sometimes," She and Peter laughed. I sat there until Peter told one of his maids to bring me some breakfast; I was so hungry I didn't refuse. They brought back French toast with eggs and two pieces of bacon. Yum-my, I guess I'll dig in Kristen.

"So Kristen, you and Drake are going to be leaving at noon today in one of my private jets," I looked at him, one of his private jets. Damn, I guess.

"Yea, okay," I just sat and ate.

"Honey, you need to start packing. Sandra can help you out," My mom said as she patted my hand.

"After I'm done eating," I grumbled, to my surprise Peter chuckled.

"I think she's right on this one, let her finish her meal." And with that, I didn't think Peter was such an asshole as I thought him out to be.

I went to my room after I was done with my delicious breakfast, I rubbed my eyes. My god I needed more sleep. I passed the bathroom but crushed into his hard chest. I raised my head, I found Drake smiling down at me, I realized my hands were spread across his stomach, a very detailed muscularly stomach.

"Good morning to you too," He said and smiled down at me, I moved away as fast as I could.

"Watch where you're going," I said, as I walked away.

"You are the one who bumped into me, don't I deserve an apology?" He asked, and I found myself turning toward him in anger.

"I need to apologize; in my opinion you bumped into me!" I stared back waiting for an answer.

"Whatever makes you sleep at night," he smirked. I turned around, I knew I was right. No need to prove my point to someone like him.

"Kristen," he called behind me,

"What?" He came close, I didn't move, he caught me off guard, he then moved his hand behind me and tapped my ass, my whole body became hot, and there was such a yearning that shot up my spine. No! Body, please stop reacting like this! I pushed him away so hard he stumbled.

He was laughing; he raised his hands up, smiled, and said "You're wet from behind, thought I let you know."

Oh right, I sat on that damn wet spot this morning, Shit! Curse my mother.

"So, why the hell did you smack my ass?" I yelled.

"I didn't smack it, I tapped it. He said." I hate him!

"Same damn thing!" I turned around and just kept walking.

I entered my room without hesitation and jumped onto the bed. It was no longer wet; I guess the maids must have changed the sheets. The door opened and Sandra walked in.

"Hey, your mom asked me to help you pack."

"Ugh! I don't want to pack, I need my beauty sleep."

"You had enough sleep, c'mon. The faster we pack the sooner you will be on the island." She said matter-of-factly.

"Fine, whatever" I took out my suit case and started packing again. I only had some of my favorite clothes that Daniel brought back from Florida this morning.

"Okay, you just have to take this with you, it be criminal if you didn't," I looked at Sandra, she had one of my favorite two piece bikini, it was a Victoria Secret baby blue striped one. Rather sexy I must say. I looked at her.

"What about it? I'm not going to take it with me." I closed my bag to make my point. There was no way in hell Drake was seeing me in it, Period.

"Fine, whatever you say." There was knocking at the door soon followed by my mom barging in. She was wearing a banana republic skirt that reached a little over her knees and a crème blouse. Some people would actually say she looked like me, who knows what the hell they're thinking.

"Ready honey," She asked as she moved close to see if I was finished packing my stuff.

"Unfortunately, yes," Daniel came in and took my bag. Thank goodness, that thing was heavy.

"Let's go," I said. By now there is nothing I can say to get myself out of this. I may as well play along.

Chapter 6

I walked out of the mansion and got into one of the cars waiting outside. I got in still looking out of the window and saw Sandra walking toward the car. She smiled down at me and I returned the favor.

"You have to call me every single day your over there, you got it," I rolled my eyes at her and smiled.

"Sure thing Sandra,"

"I'm not kidding; I have to know all the juicy information." She winked and gave me a hug,

"For the record there will be no juicy news Sandra, so forget it."

"Sure, sure," She laughed.

"Bye,"

"Bye," as I watched her walk away, and then saw I my mom walking up; I turned around and rolled up the window. She tapped it; I rolled it down two inches.

"Good luck honey, see you in two months." She blew me a kiss; I grabbed it mid-air and pretended to break it.

"Good bye mother."

She walked away. I huffed; I wasn't going to see her for the next two months. Yippee for me, yeah right.

I saw Drake coming out of the front doors, he was wearing dark denim jeans with a grey t-shirt and had his hair tousled. Delicious, I thought suddenly. How the hell did I end up thinking that, well it wasn't a lie? He did look unbearably handsome.

He got into the car a few minutes later and settled himself into the seat close to me. "Hello gorgeous," He smiled as he fastened his seatbelt.

"Oh shut up," I mumbled, he wasn't going to start with me again. Not after his little stunt this morning.

"I'm trying to give you a compliment and this is what I get," He nodded his head from right to left.

"I don't take it as a compliment," I said as he scooted over to get closer to me, I did the opposite.

"How would you take it?" He asked me, with a small smile.

"Sexual harassment," I crossed my arms over my chest. He tapped his heart, as if to calm it down.

"Kristen, that hurts you know,"

"No I don't know. I'm not a molester."

"You have no idea who you're messing with Kristen." He joked. I snorted,

"Oh I'm so scared," I wiggled my hands around, pretending to be a ghost. He laughed and said,

"You have nerve Kristen, I like it."

"For now" I smirked and before I knew it we were out of the driveway and approaching the freeway.

Drake's POV:

Within 20 minutes of driving Kristen was well into sleeping. I studied her; she was listening to her I-pod and was sound asleep. She was wearing some sweats and a tank top under a thin American eagle sweater, that left her neck uncovered. Wow, she looked amazing, and I was so tempted. I wanted to kiss her so bad! I moved near to her lips, they were calling me. Drake, Drake. Kiss me, kiss me. They looked adorably delicious. Now, calm yourself Drake, she is just another girl. I'm not easy was ringing in the back of his mind, as she previously stated. Yea, yea right she's not just another girl.

About a half hour had passed when we arrived at the airport. I smiled to myself; we use to come here every summer for vacation. By the time I was 11 I had practically traveled to every hot spot on the globe. Lucky me, huh! I turned around to look at Kristen thinking the sound of the planes had awakened her, to my surprise she lay there just as she was before. I laughed; damn she's a heavy sleeper.

"Kristen, babe, we're here," I shoved her lightly.

"Don't call me that," she moved to a better position. "And if we're not actually here, you had better start running for your dear life."

"Feisty little dragon, aren't you. Since you don't like it, babe it is."

I don't understand; she should be all up on me by now, I must be losing my game I told myself. I didn't understand Kristen she was giving hard to get a whole new meaning.

"Fine," she yawned and looked passed me to the runway.

She grabbed her bag and swung it over her shoulder. It looked heavy; I went around the car to help with the bag.

"Hey! Give it back, "She told me. Like I said I didn't get her, here I was trying to keep her from breaking her back and all she wants is the bag back; interesting, very interesting.

"It looked heavy, I thought I would help," I shrugged, trying to make it seem like no big deal.

"Fine, have it your way." She walked passed me, suddenly I wanted her to start arguing with me again. Just to hear her voice. Wow Drake, great, just great. Now you're acting corny, way to go.

"What, no yelling or screaming?" I could feel a smile tugging at the corners of my mouth.

"No, to tell you the truth my back was killing me. So you're just doing me a favor." She shrugged and kept walking to the jet.

"So no 'Thank you' or anything," I smirked,

"Thanks," she said but her eyes turned to slits, "For now."

We got into the jet and I looked around; nothing has changed in the slightest. I looked at Kristen, and as soon as she hit the seat she positioned herself with the I-pod and began to go back to sleep. I laughed; she probably had a rough night.

Kristen's POV:

As soon as I got on jet I sat on the most comfortable looking seat and went to sleep. I didn't care if Drake had the less comfortable one; he wasn't awakened with a cold bucket of water. My mind focused on him calling me babe. It sounded so enticing. I inhaled, trying to clear away thoughts of his tempting chest and gorgeous tousled hair. Just go to sleep Kristen, I said to myself.

It seemed like I had barely closed my eyes when I felt someone shoving me from my sleep, I groaned, not again!

"What now?" I said half conscious,   "It's been such a short time," I moaned again.

Drake looked at me with an amused expression, "Kristen we've been in the air for the past two hours," he said with a laugh. Sure we have. I looked around for my things and realized they weren't there.

"Where's my stuff," I asked as I looked around, there was nothing in sight.

"Ricky and Dominic came and took them a while ago." He told me, as he began rising from his seat.

"Who the hell are they?" I needed my things, and now.

He laughed, "Easy there, they just came to take our luggage to the boat. No big deal."

"We're going on a boat?" I asked surprised.

"You don't expect us to land on the island, no runway, remember." He grabbed his bag and headed out. I started to panic. I didn't know my way around here, what if I get lost. Breathe in breath out. Drake stuck his head back into the jet and smiled.

"You are coming?" He asked.

I know I looked really worried, and all he could do was nod his head. When I reached the bottom of the stairs, I was surprised by the most beautiful view. It was about noon and the sun caused the horizon to look spectacular. Pinks, and yellows, and oranges all mixed composed the most wonderful sight. This awesome picture reflected against the ocean, mirroring it. It was just amazing. Drake came next to me. Our shoulders touched and sent an electric current through my body. Suddenly I felt safe.

"You ready to go." I turned around to find Drake staring down at me. His soft green eyes had me mesmerized me for a minute.

"Guess so," I turned around and began walking towards the docks. He caught up with me and walked along silently. The first thing I was going to do when I reached that damn island was get into bed and make best friend with a pillow. I was so tired. I couldn't believe Drake; we could not have been in the jet for two hours, it felt like only a minute.

As we got closer to the docks I noticed a small yacht coming into sight. I sighed; this little venture just wouldn't be complete without a yacht. I guess Drake heard me because he said, "What? Not good enough for you," I glared at him.

"Nah, not really" I teased. Of course it was good enough. He laughed. I entered and sat on a leather seat. Oh, and comfortable indeed. I saw Drake sit opposite of me as he reclined back into the seat. He looked so sexy; I just could not believe it. He then put his hands behind his head; those muscles were incredible. I guess the sun was bothering him because he put on some aviator glasses. Oh yeah, a sight for sore eyes. He smiled over at me.

"Are you checking' me out babe?"

I looked at him in shock, realizing that he was watching me all the time. Only he'll never know that.

"No! I was just admiring the view," I said quickly.

"You're a terrible liar Kristen," as he looked back with smiled a flirty smile.

"No I'm not," I needed to defend myself. He smiled at me seductively,

"Prove it," He challenged me.

"I don't need to prove anything to you Drake." The boat began to move away from the docks and headed fast toward an island straight ahead; my new home for the next two months.

"If that's the way you want it babe," He leaned back again, as if saying this conversation was over. I hated him.

"I told you not to call me that," I knew I had told him specifically not to call me that, well not really. But still.

"You don't like it?" He asked as he leaned in closer.

"No," He wasn't getting what he wanted and that was the end.

"Then it stays," He leaned back again. I sighed, he was impossible.

We were in the boat for a few more minutes when we finally stopped. I opened my eyes, not that I was sleeping. I just didn't want to see Drake and his fine self. I stood up and eyed around. The small island was so breathtaking. By now it was already night, but the moonlight made the sand sparkle. It looked soft and smooth. You could see the darkness behind a little beach house in the distance. I exited the yacht and felt around the sand. Yea I was right, the sand was so soft, and it almost felt as if no one had ever stepped here before. I walked to the beach house; it had a large porch, like a large cabin but it looked small. I saw Drake walking to the house as well. I went inside, thinking I could get the better bed before him. It had a small kitchen, with expensive electronics, and a small but cozy living room.

"Not too shabby," I murmured to myself. I heard the front door open and suspected that Drake came in.

I finally found a room and checked it out. It had a large king size bed, and its own private bathroom. Yeah! I wasn't going to have to share a bathroom with Drake. But that was weird why would someone alone need a king size bed. I got out the room and looked around. There was just this bedroom. Oh Shit! Please, please don't tell me.

"Drake, there's a problem." I yelled as he came into the room.

"What's wrong?" he asked as he put down the luggage.

"There's only one bedroom." I said.

"So what's the problem," He asked.

You have got to be kidding me! "That means there's only one bed!" I almost screamed. I saw a mischievous smile form in the tips of his mouth.

"I don't see how that's a problem." His smile had reached its peak!

Chapter 7

"I do!" I screamed and slammed the door right in his perfect face. He wasn't going to sleep in the same bed with me, not now not ever.

"Kristen, c'mon open the door, I'm fucking tired." I could even see him smiling.

"That makes two of us, and no, you can sleep in the damn living room." I said crossing my arms across my chest.

"Well it's my house, and I'm the boss around here," He joked around.

"What's mine is yours, remember honey!" I told him. Ha! He ate his own words, moron!

"Touché babe, I'm impressed," He knocked on the door again, gently this time.

"Just go sleep in the living room, there's a first for everything,"

"I'll behave," He said.

"I don't believe you," My voice left an echo around the room.

"Fine, see you in the morning." What, he wasn't going to persist, he must really be tired.

I turned on the light and looked around; it was a pretty big room. Long curtains adorn the windows. There was a big closet, creamy carpet and a bathroom with a huge Jacuzzi bathtub. I looked around for my stuff so I can get my cozy pajamas, but my bag was not to be found. I looked around the big room and then I realized Drake must have brought it in, and it was left in the living room. Damn! I turned off the lights and held my breath; and slowly, so slowly began to open the door. I looked around outside, it was dark; the only light was from the moon. I sighed; I could hear the waves crashing back and forth on the shore. It sounded like home.

I spotted my bag, but then I also noticed Drake's. Curiosity washed over me and I decided to take a look. I opened it slightly and caught sight of a book. It was a real heavy book, I picked it up and read the title, 'Physics for Scientists and Engineers: A Strategic Approach By: Randall D. Knight.' Wow, not so bad. Maybe he's not so much of a dumbass, maybe he wants to make something with of his life. I put the book down and closed the bag trying not to make much noise, or so I thought.

"What you looking for babe?" Drake asked as he sat up from a shirtless sleep. Damn, nice. C'mon, breathe Kristen, open your mouth and speak. But I couldn't, my eyes were glued to his chest, those chiseled abs and muscles.

"Nothing," I said after my recovery.

"Kristen, you do realize I've been awake since you got out the bedroom door." His eyes were smiling but his mouth was set into a serious line.

"Of course I did," I lied.

"What were you doing snooping through my stuff?" He stood up and came closer to me. The moon gave him an angel sort of glow. He looked fine as hell, I might add.

I sighed, he saw me, no use denying it.

"Fine, I was curious. I came to get my bag and yours was slightly opened. So don't blame me, blame my curiosity." I finished and looked down to the floor with my bag next to me. By now Drake was standing right in front of me. Leaving only the air we breathe to separate us.

"Curiosity killed the cat, ever heard of that," He smiled.

"Yea I have." What was he saying; was he going to kill me. Ha! Sure he was.

"Oh well, no big deal. I searched through yours as well." He shrugged and went back to lie down on the futon. I felt my face growing hot again.

"You what," I yelled. He raised his head and looked at me mischievously.

"Nice panties" and he winked.

"You disrespectful bastard" I said. I grabbed my bag and went to my bedroom.

"It's only fair babe," I heard him say. I slammed the door hard enough to make the mirror rattle.

Drake's POV:

I laughed quietly to myself when she slammed the door. She can sure get worked up, can't she? Just like her, curiosity was killing me when I saw the lace protruding from the pocket of her suitcase. God knows, I wanted to see her in them so bad it hurt. She had a marvelously sculpted ass, not like I was watching; I mean every time I looked around, there it was.

I had not planned on confessing to looking in her bags, hell no, I probably wouldn't even be here this moment. She probably would have kicked my ass if she had not been caught going through my bags.

Guilt overcame me. Damn, I was helpless under those little cute pouting lips. It was settled, in the morning I was going to apologize to her.

I woke up sore from sleeping in that uncomfortable futon. I rubbed my eyes and went to the bathroom to take a leak. I brushed my teeth as well. As soon as I got out of the bathroom I saw Kristen in the kitchen. I looked over at the clock on the wall. It was only 10:23 a.m., why the hell was she up so early, I mean, for her it seemed early.

I walked toward the kitchen but stopped at the island counter, thinking that Kristen might still be upset from the night before. I wouldn't want to be near her when knives are around.

"Good morning," I said. Her eyes turned to slits when she saw me, but then her eyes fell to my stomach. Those eyes widened a bit then, I smiled broadly and opened my arms.

"You want to touch," I laughed at the look on her face, she was blushing. Holy fuck! Kristen blushing, now there's a first. Oh well, it was fun while it lasted. As soon as she recovered, those eyes immediately went back to the glaring look of hatred that was growing on me.

"No! That's the last thing I want to do, get away from me!" She said and backed away. She was lying. She wanted me.

"Fine," I looked over to the beach, it looked so inviting. I turned to Kristen, finding that she too was staring at the ocean.

"You want to go for a swim?" I asked pointing at the nice warm waves.

"No, I'm fine." She grabbed a bag of Hash Browns from the LG refrigerator. I stared at her.

"Don't be such a lazy ass; you know you want to go." I went around her and grabbed her arms, making swimming motions with them. She froze but didn't flinch. I could feel heat bouncing off from her skin. She skin smelled so good, like roses straight from a garden. I looked down into her face and could see her smiling, a small dimple surfaced from her cheek. She had a beautiful smile. It was intoxicating; she made me smile as well.

"You're right; I shouldn't be a lazy ass." She agreed with me. I laughed, thinking I could get use to this.

"I'm sorry for going through your stuff last night that was a mistake." Her face softened, but looked very serious.

"Yea it was, but I did the same, so you're forgiven." She gave in.

"I don't get a 'sorry,' "I asked with the best doggy face I could get together. She pushed me away and smiled an inch.

"Don't push your luck Drake," I love the way she said my name for some strange reason.

"Fine, but look on the bright side, you could show off your hot body with that striped Victoria's Secret bikini," as I smiled. She turned around, unbelief mixed with anger rose from her face. Fuck, what did I do this time?

Chapter 8

"Kristen, what's wrong?" Drake asked. I guess I looked pretty mad, Sandra that weasel, what did I ask her not to do. Don't pack this bikini, and what does she do. Pack this bikini. I started to stomp to my room like a little spoiled brat, Drake started to follow.

"Kristen what the hell is wrong with you, I said I was sorry didn't I? Damn, somebody must be bipolar." He said. What the hell, I'm not bipolar. I'm an outgoing person, a laid back kind of girl. But around him my emotions turn to mush.

"I am not bipolar," I kept walking until I reached the room. I decided it was time to unpack. I grabbed my suitcase and slammed it on the bed. I didn't realize that the front pocket was opened, and guess what fell out; yes those darn condoms. Ugh! Thanks to my dumbass mother and her brilliant plans. I reached for them as fast as I could, praying that Drake hadn't noticed. Too bad, God wasn't on my side today. Drake smiled so wide, it looked like his face was going to crack. He grabbed the two that fell out and laughed.

"It would be a shame if we didn't get to use them." He came closer, and smiled seductively.

"Well too bad for you. I'm not as easy as those other girls you sleep with," I said. He was so close I could smell his cologne. He smelled so good, it was hard to resist going over to him and licking it off. Ugh Kristen, you pervert.

He laughed, "Kristen, you make it seem like I have sex every night with different girls. For your information, I don't. And my kind of girl has to be smart as well as beautiful." He said it matter-of-factly.

"Big difference," I said, walking right by him to get outside. Wow, the ocean looks more beautiful every time I see it. Caribbean blues mixed with green. It was so inviting, I couldn't help myself. I needed a swim, without Drake checking me out of course. I began smiling without my own permission; I really did like the idea of him checking me out.

"So are you a virgin?" I heard a masculine voice sounding behind me. I turned around and saw Drake coming out with a white shirt and some jeans. God Drake why did you have to cover your chest?

"Why not ask me something more, I don't know, personal?" I turned back around to appreciate the wonderful view.

"You're my fiancé, I think I need to know this," He looked over at me.

"I won't tell you, why not ask me what's my favorite color or something?" Out of all the questions he could ask me, this is what he asks. How typical.

"I already know all that, you mom already told that stuff." He said. "Your favorite color's light blue. Your favorite hobby's running and you like to stuff your mouth with cheerios, anything I miss?" He said and walked over next to me.

"Oh my mom gave you the general stuff." I turned to look at him, his eyes locked with mine. His eyes blended into a beautiful picture, he smiled at me and leaned in closer to me. I had to snap out of it. Control Kristen, control. I backed away slightly.

"No, I'm not," Why the hell was I telling him this? Oh well, it's out of my mouth now. He smiled victorious,

"Really, Saint Kristen you're not a virgin. That's hard to believe." He laughed. I might be a good person, but I am no saint.

"Really, you're the fucking pro around here, so when did you lose it huh?" Damn show-off. I could be wild when I wanted to be. I just wanted to prove a point.

"15. But I could ask you the same question babe."

"16, there, are you happy now?" All he did was laugh. What an asshole.

"Oh yeah looks like there's a devil inside you after all, I'm impressed." I glared at him and began walking towards the beach. With his speed he grabbed my wrist and turned me into him. I was now plastered onto his chest. His smell was overwhelming, I wanted him. Now!

"Why don't you leave me alone Drake," I asked in a whisper.

"I tried, but as you can see, no such luck." He smiled a warm smile. I looked away afraid that if I looked back into those eyes I couldn't help myself.

"Fine, looks like it's up to me." I untangled my hands away from his and ran back towards the house. I went straight to my room. Why am I feeling this way, those eyes, I sighed; those fucking eyes could be the death of me. I needed to get my thoughts straight. The only thing that came to mind was a shower. Yeah, let me go and take a shower. I grabbed some clothes and headed for the bathroom. Drake was nowhere to be seen. Good. I laid my clothes to the side and began to undress. I turned on the shower to hottest temperature; I stepped inside and began to shampoo. No guy, as I recall has ever made me feel this way. Made me feel safe and wanted. No one else could give me this type of sensation; this is so unfamiliar to me. Only Drake could.

I couldn't fall for him, I just couldn't. I have heard the rumors about broken hearts and I don't want to be next. I can't let that happen to me. Drake seems like the type of guy that all those rumors were about. He had a dangerous type of appeal, you know, with that Greek God look and that over flirtatious attitude. I sighed, I can't even help myself. I walked over to turn off the water and slipped on a piece of soap. Damn it!

Drake's POV:

"Ah," I heard a scream from the inside the house, what had Kristen done this time? I ran in, my heart beating out of control in my chest. I looked around the house, but noticed steam coming from the bathroom door. I turned the doorknob a couple times. Shit! It was locked.

"Kristen, are you alright!" I pushed against the door. I sighed, it wasn't working. I took a few steps back and kicked the door with all the power I could gather. The door opened and I rushed inside. Kristen yelped as soon as she saw me. Whoa. She had a small towel covering her womanhood, but the rest she was covering with her arm. I stared with my eyes searching hungrily around her body. Her cleavage provoked extreme temptation and her skin was glowing. Damn, I could feel my manhood growing hard. Since when did cleavage arouse me like this? Wow, she was absolutely beautiful. She had wonderful legs and her skin, and what a wonderful tan. My eyes rose to look at her face. Her eyes full of shock and unbelief. Her eyes began to move down my body and stopped at the mass beneath my abs. Her eyes widened.

"Drake, get the fuck out!" She screamed, but I was frozen. She looked around and grabbed a shampoo bottle. Brace yourself Drake, here it comes. She threw it at me with such force I tumbled and quickly snapped out of it. "Oh, Kristen, calm the hell down!"

"Just get out Drake!" She looked around again and decided this time she was going to throw the conditioner. Hell no she wasn't. I ran out the bathroom as fast as I could. I closed the door and heard a thump afterwards. I rubbed my forehead. Ouch, that was going to hurt tomorrow.

Kristen's POV:

The door shut, I looked at it not knowing what had just happened. I exhaled; if he had come sooner he would have seen me naked. Since when was I such a klutz? A bar of soap, are you kidding me, a bar of soap. My cell phone rang. I dried off my hands to answer my phone.

"Hello," I said.

"So tell me, anything good happened yet?" I heard Sandra's distant voice.

"Nothing Sandra" My back ached; I was going to need a bag full of ice.

"Don't lie, I could tell you're out of breath. C'mon Kristen I won't tell" She laughed excitedly. Then I remembered what that little back-stabber did to me.

"Sandra, why the hell did you pack that damn bikini?"

She giggled, "That wasn't me, innocent until proven guilty."

"My ass you're innocent, you know I am always tempted to wear it! I swear when I get home... you had better start running!"

"Kristen, you know you love me. Besides when you get home you're going to be thanking me."

"I highly doubt that, bye."

Chapter 9

A week passed without much communication at the beach house. I guess it's because of the incident last week; you could say it was really awkward. I guess it's just me. I've been trying to avoid coming into contact with him. In other words, I was traumatized. My stomach growled all of a sudden, I groaned. Drake was in the kitchen stuffing his mouth with food. I had to do what had what I had to do. I walked to the door and peeked out looked around. Good, no one in sight, I sighed in relief. I tried to tip-toe my way to the small but extravagant kitchen but quickly stopped when I saw Drake with a sub in his hands. I immediately turned around and started to walk quickly back to my room.

"Kristen, hold up!" He said coming after me. I power-walked faster to my room but he soon caught up with me.

"Kristen, I'm going crazy! As you may notice I'm a very social person, and that means I go insane without someone to talk with. You haven't exactly been the best company over the past week. So please I'm begging, talk to me woman!" He shook me from by the shoulders expecting an answer.

"You just broke into the bathroom, by kicking the door open while I was in the shower. You saw me half naked! What am I supposed to do?" He moved his arms down my shoulder and began rubbing his chin thoughtfully.

"Well, I guess you have a point. You know what though," he asked me with his fingers still in his beautifully shaped chin.

"What's that?" I positioned my hands on my hips, challenging him.

"You should be thanking me," he said and smiled. I was becoming angry, no that's not what I should be doing. I should be drowning his ass.

"Listen. I was just being a good friend; after all I thought something was wrong when I heard the scream. I was just checking to make sure you weren't dying on me." Drake mimicked my posture and smiled. I processed this information; and maybe he did have a point. I sighed, yes he did.

"Fine, you have a point. Thanks for trying to help me;" I laughed and continued, "I think I still have a bruise from the fall."

He laughed along with me, "I have an idea," He said, his eyes started to sparkle the way they did when he had something up his sleeve.

"What might that be?" Seriously what can it be, I was clueless at that moment.

"I'll make you some dinner, you know, to make it up to you." His hands formed into the begging position. And he looked so cute doing it. Yes he did, so stop denying it Kristen, I thought to myself.

"I don't know," I said, but my stomach grumbled in disagreement. Drake with his sharp senses heard it as well.

"Your stomach doesn't seem to think so," Damn him and those wonderful senses! But again, he had a point.

"Fine you caught me. Let's go eat." I gave in, he smiled a victorious smile. He grabbed my hand and led me to the kitchen. When our hands met, that mere touch sent electricity through my body once again. Unknown feelings, I always lighted up around Drake. He sat me in one of the bar stools at the kitchen bar. I sat without hesitation and looked at him with excitement.

"So what are we having?" My stomach growled some more.

"Dominic came this the morning and brought us some food." A bag was on the island counter. Drake went over and began to open it.

"Surprise, surprise, we're having...hamburgers." He sighed, "Why couldn't they bring some fish or something native from around here? Damn, I guess 'cause they know we're American, they have to bring American food." He looked at the food in disapproval.

I laughed, "You're adventurous aren't you?" He looked at me in surprise; I guess he wasn't expecting my comment.

"Yea I guess you can say that, I am rather adventurous." He moved to the cabinets and took out two glass plates and two glass cups. He came and placed the cup in front of me and laid the hamburger onto the plate. His marvelous scent lingered. I inhaled; yummy I will never get tired of that smell.

"So where are we?" I asked, I've been wondering for ages. As soon as he sat down he smiled and answered.

"We're on Bladen Island of the Marshall Islands, but that's not what we call it." He took a huge bite off his hamburger; he looked like a blowfish, a very handsome blowfish.

"What do you call it?" My curiosity started to boil inside me.

"Marjorie Island. We renamed the island after my mom when she passed away." He took another bite, but sadness reflected from his eyes. I regretted pushing this issue.

"I'm sorry," was all I could say. I felt bad for Drake. I mean, I fight with my mom tirelessly but she is my best friend. Well beside Sandra.

"It's okay, it's been a while," He shrugged it off, but sadness still lingered in his usually cheerful eyes.

"Marjorie's a very pretty name Drake," My voice turned soft. His smile was forced a bit but he nodded in agreement.

"Her dad was French. When I was little I had to bury myself in a French text book all day long. She really wanted me to learn the language." He chuckled at the memory and turned his head around to look at me.

"So what's your story babe?" He wondered. I sipped some of my Sprite and answered.

"My dad left us when right after I was born and my mom had to raise me by herself. I don't count the boyfriends she had over the years." Nope, they were nothing to me. I guess you could call them my Moms little puppets. Nothing really lasted with my Mom.

"That must have been hard on you," He sounded sincere, I turned and smiled.

"It wasn't such a big deal really. They never lasted longer than two months." I told him. I took another bite of my burger; I didn't want to talk about it anymore.

"So Sandra's your best friend huh?" Of course he noticed Sandra.

"Yup, my very best friend, we've been together since babies. Her mom and mine were college buddies. They kind of raised us together; they got knocked up around the same time, and Sandra was born about a week before me." How weird, my mom getting knocked up, right!

"Interesting story, how old are you Kristen?" He smirked.

"I'm 25," I said, sighing dramatically. He laughed at me,

"You are a fucking liar Kristen, how old are you really?" He finished his burger a whole mouthful ago. I had a long way to go.

"I'm 19," I gave in. He smirked.

"Not too bad," He nodded up and down.

"So how old are you Casanova?" He couldn't be much older than me to tell you the truth.

"Take a guess,"

I looked around the kitchen; hmmm maybe something could give me an idea.

"Uh, about... 27" I slightly squinted my eyes in doubt. He nodded his head in disagreement and put on a wide smile.

"Do I look that old to you? You disappoint me babe."

"Fine...umm...26...no? Fine, let's see....24?" He stopped me right there.

"Your horrible at guessing Kristen, I'll put you out of your misery. I'm actually...21" He grinned at me. I laughed. Wow, I wasn't so far off. He was just making it a big deal.

"Your two years older than me. But I guess you could say I'm older in the maturity area." I said. I was, in no question more mature than Drake. He smirked.

"It's called having fun, it's not my fault you are such a moody little girl." He scrambled my hair the way adults do little children.

"I'm not moody; I can have a little fun when I want to. You're the one that gets moody, and I'm not a little girl." My chest puffed out as if to make a point.

"Whatever you say babe, in other words, you're a spoilsport," He laughed hard and caused the bar stool to shake. I punched him lightly in his arm,

"I am NOT a spoilsport" I said between laughs. He laughed harder, he had contagious laughter. I laughed along with him.

"Sure you're not babe." He told me, "You're not as bad as you seem. You could actually take a joke, and here I thought you were bipolar." His knee and mine ended up touching as we went with our conversation. He was facing me cheerful face.

"I told you I am not bipolar, you need to get that through your brainless head." I tapped his head, and smiled.

"For your information babe, I did well in school, unlike some people in this room." His eyes looked at me.

I looked around and pointed a finger at myself, "Are you talking about me?" I asked innocently. He rolled his eyes.

"Who else to you see around here smart-ass" He snickered. I giggled.

"I do well in school; I don't know who the hell told you I didn't."

"I'm smarter," He informed me. I laughed.

"There is no way in burning hell you're smarter than me Drake, that's a fact." He wasn't and that was it.

"Whatever helps you sleep at night babe," I looked at him with an expression that I guess was pretty amusing because he started to laugh so hard he finally made the stool tumble over. Before I knew it he grabbed my hand and pulled me along with him. I landed hard on his chest, I groaned. I raised my head and found my eyes looking into those green eyes. I didn't want to move away from his clutches, but it had to be done. As soon as I got up I pulled his hand to help him up. When I did, he came to his feet and peered at me in amazement. "Sorry about that, I'm a spontaneous type of person."

I began laughing but was soon interrupted by Drake's lips crushing onto mines. Yea, he was indeed spontaneous.

Chapter 10

His lips molded perfectly with mine. They were soft and they tasted so delicious, I was wondering if I would ever get tired of kissing them. Too bad I couldn't investigate. My hands curled with handfuls of his soft hair and pulled him closer. His smell was so intoxicating that it made me want him even more. He moved back and looked down at me. My eyes were still closed; I didn't want to wake up from this wonderful dream.

"Told you, I knew you wanted me, babe." He whispered seductively in my ear. My hands were still in his hair so I decided to take advantage of it. I pulled his smooth hair and said...

"You're way too cocky for my taste, you know." I teased him. He looked at me as if I said he smelled bad. But it's Drake, so of course he took it as a challenge.

"And you're way too much of a fun-sucker for my taste. How is it that you drive me crazy?" He asked himself. I like that idea. I made him crazy.

"Because I have that effect in people" I walked around him, my finger tracing every muscle through his shirt. He laughed and caught my wrist. He pulled me close to him until I was inches away from that handsome face.

"Now whose being cocky babe," I leaned into him, wanting a kiss. He got the message and started to pucker those juicy lips of his. Before he could touch mine, I pulled away and started heading for my bedroom. His eyes fluttered open and started to chase me. I giggled loudly and started to dart faster.

"You can run but sooner or later, I'm going to get you!" I heard him yell behind me.

I looked back and saw him a few feet away. I threw my hands in the air and started to really run faster. Shit, he was fast. I darted out the front door and started to run towards the beautiful sea, the horizon lingering in its waves. I ran until I fell into the sand, as I was breathing deeply from running. Drake laughed in victory. He pulled me to him and wrapped his arms around my waist.

"Gotcha," He smiled widely at me. My knees became weak, who knows if it was from running or because of the gorgeous man holding me tightly against his chest.

"You are such...a...damn...cheater...Drake Montréal," I said between breaths.

"How the hell am I a cheater, Kristen?" He grabbed a lose strand of my hair and gently tucked it in behind my ear.

"You have long-ass legs." I finally got my breathing to get back to normal. I pulled away and started to walk toward the ocean. He followed and said…

"It's not my fault I'm a natural born athlete." I snickered and threw some salt water at him.

"There, wake up, because your dreaming." I turned around and enjoyed the miraculous view. It was soon interrupted by Drake's splashes as he walked near to me.

"Let's go for a swim babe, I now you have been dying to try it out."

"Maybe your right just let me go and change." I ran to the house but realized Drake was still in his jeans.

"You are not going to change?" I asked him.

"I don't take an hour to get ready; I'll stay out here for a little while longer." I rolled my eyes and started to power-walked to the house. The bedroom door was opened and I walked in with haste. I looked around for my bag, oh here it is. I began digging for the well-known Victoria Secret masterpiece. Aha, here's my striped masterpiece of a bikini. I strolled into the bathroom and started to put it on. The bikini outlined my curves better than any other bikini I had ever worn. Of course, that's the reason I love it so much. Maybe Sandra was right, maybe I was going to be thanking her. I threw my clothes into a bucket in the corner of the room and started to walk bare-foot from the house.

My eyes scanned the beach for Drake. I found him sitting by a palm tree. I was surprised to see him in his swim trunks already. I walked to him; his head shot up fast and looked at me with his eyes widened slightly. The corners of my mouth pulled up into a smile. That's the reaction I always got when I wore this bikini. Score one for Kristen.

He stood up and smiled his famous smile at me.

"You look...you have...beautiful." He said looking a little dazed. My feet started to walk closer to him. I poked him in his well defined stomach and pointed towards the ocean.

"It is getting dark. Hurry before the sunlight runs out." I turned around and started heading for the water. I wasn't going to wait for him to answer. The soft hot sand filled the gaps between my toes, massaging them with its texture as I kept walking.

"You love the ocean, huh babe." He said from behind.

"I guess you can say that. I grew up with the beach as my neighbor; I guess I've grown rather fond of it over the years." I kept walking, dodging waves as they hit me. I stopped when the water came to my chest; soon I dived into the water with ease. The warm water covered every inch of my body. I was in heaven, the tides began to move me and my feet automatically navigated through them. A few seconds later, I came to swim to the surface. I inhaled deeply and looked around.

Drake was a few feet away, his hair wet and tousled. He looked absolutely marvelous, the moon's glow reflecting off his skin. He walked toward me, ignoring the waves that were pushing him back. He stood in front of me, his strong arms pulling me into him.

"Aphrodite doesn't come close." He whispered into my hair. I laughed and said,

"Don't let her hear you; she might turn me into a repulsive troll." I told him.

"She'd have to go through me. I can be Hercules when I want to be." He said as I giggled. Why have I been giggly around him lately? Why does my heart quicken at the sight of him? Why do I want to laugh and smile every time he does? I knew Drake was all sorts of trouble, and yet I still felt and attraction towards him. Why? Who knows? Who cares?

"Oh really, prove it." I challenged him. He smiled widely and grabbed my waist. He threw me over his cold shoulders and began walking up to the shore. I squealed and started laughing. My numb hands slapped his back.

"Stop squirming Kristen!" He told me loudly so his voice could be heard over the loud waves.

"Please don't! And would you please put me down, I'm getting seriously dizzy." Ugh, I was going to be sick if he didn't put me down soon. Drake placed me gently on a big rock next to the shore. I started to massage my temples, making me feel better in an instant.

"Was that enough to prove you wrong?" He asked me.

"Nope, sorry Hercules" He laughed and sat next to me. He rested his head on top of mine. It felt so normal, like we've been doing it forever.

"You're a hard person to please babe." He said while taking my hands into his.

"So I've been told." I sighed. It's true, I've always been told that I was either picky or just a hard to please person. But that was me.

"I'm not the only one?" He raised an eyebrow at me.

"Nope, you're probably the...umm...I lost count, to tell you the truth." He smiled radiantly and said,

"Everyone's different Kristen. You should take it as a compliment, not an insult." He said. I smiled up at him. I was surprised at how smart he sounded.

"Maybe you're right Buddha." I chuckled. He nodded and raised my hand up to his lips and kissed it lightly.

"You should listen to me more often babe," he said. I turned my face to look at him.

"No I shouldn't," I responded. He leaned in closer to me, his face inches from mine.

"I always know best." He tilted my chin and before I could respond his lips came softly to mine. My body surrendered to his touch and I was left without any control. He parted his sweet lips from mine way to soon. I admit I was disappointed. Why was it that when I didn't want to kiss him, he would give a long and delicious one? And when I wanted a kiss it was just a peck. A damn peck!

"We should get back, it's getting cold." He stood up and stuck his hand out for me to grab on. I took it; he soon pulled me forward, pulling me into his chest. He looked at me mischievously.

"Would you like me to carry you, Ms. Whitmore?" He asked, grabbing hold of my waist.

"Yes, I would like that Hercules." I slid my hands up his neck, locking them in position. He winked at me.

"Better hold on tighter," Drake whispered loudly over the waves. I smiled and shook my head; I tightened my grip on his neck. My body now plastered onto his. Drake bent down to grab my now shivering legs and trusted them up to his arms. He walked over to the shore, with me in the safety of his grip. I rested my head onto his chest, listening to the steady beat of his heart. It seemed so peaceful, I sighed softly. It felt great to be in his arms, the mere feeling sent tranquility throughout my body; making me warm.

He settled me into the comfortable bed,

"Sweet dreams babe," He walked out the door, leaving the room silent. I was dead tired, and I knew Drake was too. I felt guilty for making him sleep on that little futon. I sighed and started to walk to the door. Drake was already lying down, getting comfortable.

"Drake, do you want to come to bed with me tonight?" I said before I could stop the words from coming out of my mouth. You wouldn't believe how fast his head shot up. He looked at me for a moment, then that grin started as he was filled with excitement. He quickly resembled a Cheshire Cat. He stood up and approached me.

He snickered, "Finally. I thought you'd never ask." I smiled to myself and led the way.

A soon as we came in Drake yawned and soon feel on top of the bed.

"Change, you're not going to sleep with your trunks are you?"

"I'll be back then, wait for me babe," He left the room.

I soon found my bags and got out my pajamas. Just a tank-top and some Juicy Couture sweat pants. I went into the bathroom and changed quickly, brushing my teeth afterwards. I looked at myself in the mirror, glad at what I saw. I sighed and turned back to the empty bedroom. Drake came in with his chest bare and some boxers hanging low on his waist. Wow, he looked enchanting. I just wanted to ravish him there in the spot. Too bad for my good self control, he looked around and began smiling again as he saw me.

"Let's get ready to rumble babe." He motioned me to the bed in the middle of the room. I rolled my eyes at him,

"Don't make me regret this decision." I told him in jest.

"Fine," He beamed. I folded the first layer of covering back and motioned for him to get in. He jumped in and patted the space next to him. I looked at him with question. He returned a reassuring smile. Stop being such a wuss Kristen, it's just one guy. Yea that's the problem; he's not just a guy. It's Drake we're talking about. Oh well, I pushed aside all my thoughts and joined him. I had to lay at the edge, still trying not to be too easy. I heard his laugh and turned over to face him.

"I'm going to trust you to behave yourself now go to sleep." I turned myself over again, but he grabbed hold of my waist, pulling me into him.

"C'mon babe, cuddle with me, I know you're cold." He said softly in my ear. I shook my head.

"That's why they invented blankets," I argued. My body tried to wiggle from his grip but couldn't. He was strong, and had one hell of a grip.

"Yea, but there's nothing compared to body heat." He said with a smile clearly in his voice. Okay, maybe he was right. Just for one night, it wouldn't hurt anybody.

"Fine, just be mature about it." I swear if he tried to do something, he would be limping tomorrow.

"Of course I will," he pulled me closer to him. Leaving his arm securely around my waist, it felt great to be here.

"Good night," He said, that was soon followed by a light kiss on my neck. I felt myself growing hot, I knew I was blushing. Thank God we turned the lights turned off.

"Good night," I responded in a whisper so low, I doubt he heard me. I closed my eyes and began to drift into blissful sleep, with Drake's arms around my waist.

Chapter 11

"Good morning sunshine." I heard as I began to awaken from a comfy night's sleep. I untangled the covers that were holding me prisoner and turned to where that masculine voice was coming from.

"Huh?" I said with a voice still sounding groggy from sleep.

"Good morning," I heard again followed by a low chuckle. My eye lids opened fully and looked at Drake. He had his whole body turned towards me, his head resting on his palm. He looked wonderful; his skin was illuminated by the sun coming in from the opened window.

"G-good morning," I stammered as I turned quickly towards for bathroom.

"Where are you going?" Drake said as he mimicked my movements. I kept walking as I opened the door.

"Where does it look like I'm going? I need to use the bathroom." I answered his ridiculous comment.

"No need for an attitude. I was just curious."

"Well remember, curiosity killed the cat," I just sounded like I had a sore throat. Drake responded with a low chuckle and then nodded in disagreement.

"I didn't sound like that. My voice was way sexier," He said with a smile, his face sparkling with amusement.

"I've heard better and besides my voice is the sexiest here." I found myself smirking.

"Whatever, you know my voice is irresistible." He laughed and wiggled his eyebrows seductively. I took this opportunity to slam the door right in his cheerful face. I huffed and walked to the sink. A squeal escaped my lips as I saw myself in the decorative mirror. I looked terrible. My hair was in knots all over my face. My eyes were somewhat red from the long sleep. You let yourself go Kristen. I thought to myself.

"What's wrong?" I heard Drake say.

"Uh... nothing, nothing, don't worry about it." I lied quickly. I turned on the water and let the warm water flow. My hands caught some water and I splashed my face. The morning was definitely not my time of day. Quite the opposite actually, by my look: morning HATED me. I sighed in relaxation and patted my face dry. A lot better than before, I can assure you. I brushed my teeth twice, and changed into suitable clothing. Some dark faded jeans and a plain gray tank-top. Go natural when on an island, right.

"Almost done there? He said."

"What's it to you?" I asked. And here I thought he was in the kitchen eating like there was no tomorrow, my mistake.

"Dominic came to drop off some desserts; I'm guessing you don't want any. That's fine, more for me." he teased, but I knew it had to be somewhat true. So I gasped and opened the door as quickly as my hand would let me.

"You must be kidding! Who said I don't want any?" I yelped. Over my dead body was he getting all the dessert?

"I just assumed…" He shrugged and grinned.

"You assumed wrong," I said, "so where's the dessert?" I asked rubbing my hands together.

He motioned his head over to the bed as he smiled. It surprised me, the bed showed no sign of our long night's slumber. On top of that, there where silver platters spread all over it. My eyes expanded as I began to smile like the Cheshire Cat.

"Paradise," I mumbled in awe at the beautiful sight before me. Nobody comes between me and my desserts. My eyes searched the bed. I found myself staring at all my favorites: chocolate truffles, crème Brule, éclairs, German cookies, chocolate mousse, napoleons, apple tarte tatin and much more. My eyes were gleaming; Drake's low chuckle disrupted my moment. I looked at him and said…

"Oh, shut up. Can't you see I'm trying to savor this moment while it lasts?" I quickly turned my head back to the marvelous spread of decorated pastries before my eyes. I sighed dreamily. I want them, I want them all and I want them now.

"Easy there. You look so crazy right now, you're scaring me Kristen." "I think we should move them to the kitchen, we sleep in here!"

"So! No problem. I can always lick the crème from the sheets." I shrugged like it was no big deal. Of course this wasn't true. I wouldn't really lick the crème from the sheets, would I? Okay, maybe if no one could see me. But most likely I wouldn't. That's type of behavior is unacceptable in my 'society.'

"Now that would be a sight to see," he winked at me. I scowled at him,

"You are so damned immature, but fine. Move them over; just be careful not to spill anything." I cautioned him. Drake walked over to the trays and began to lift them.

"You have a big-ass sweet tooth, babe." Drake smiled, he began to pile the trays one on top of the other as he carried them to the kitchen. My stomach grumbled, and I know it's bad to eat sweets in the morning: but fuck morning and those no-sweets-in-the-morning rules. I was hungry as hell and who would really pass up on this spread decadent desserts? Could you really deny this luxury? A dare would not stop you; you would accept the challenge. Eat and be happy.

"Yes I have a huge sweet tooth, but with this spread who wouldn't." I skipped happily to the kitchen after Drake gathered all the trays.

"Whoa, isn't this one really expensive?" I said as I picked up one of the truffles. I had only seen it on my last vacation to Italy. Although it looked extremely delicious, I couldn't afford it; believe it or not I could think of better things on which to spend my pocket change.

"Yea, I guess. That's what the Montreal's do, they brag about their expensive desserts. It's a waste of money in my opinion." Drake shrugged.

"Oh yeah, right, I forgot. You people are rich as hell." I sat on a bar stool and began to dig in. I began to stuff my face with everything I could reach.

"Mm, but don't be fooled, we are irresistible too."

I exhaled, "Drake, don't play with me, and don't worry, I am not falling for you," I said matter-of-factly. From the corner of my eyes I could see his face light up flirtatiously.

"You can't lie for shit Kristen. The kiss from yesterday told me all I needed to know. You know you'd do just about anything to get me in bed right now. "

I couldn't believe he was so sure about me. But he was right; my heart along with every other muscle in my body was in an uproar. I did want him, but I must be strong.

"You and your cocky ass need to get things straight." I gulped the remains of my truffle, feeling full all of a sudden.

"You're blushing. See, you have no self-control. Lucky me, don't you think?" He smirked as he started to get closer and closer.

"Fuck off." I pushed him away, even though everything inside me denied it. Rapidly I went to the bedroom, until something hooked me firmly at my waist.

"I thought we were getting along well, babe. What happened, I was joking." His hands didn't move from where they were; he just held me firmly close to his chest.

"That's because I let myself believe you were a normal person. That was my mistake, your still the same guy I met weeks ago. A cocky man-whore," I huffed.

"A man-whore, you got it all wrong." He laughed. I turned around in his grasp and clenched my arms around his neck. My eyes began to search all over face.

"I'm sure I didn't," I confirmed. His eyes softened with delight,

"Stop being a little smart-ass and kiss me." He pleaded. A slow smile began spreading around my mouth. Drake mimicked me and leaned in closer. Our lips met half way and moved rhythmically, slowly with as much passion as we could gather. His tongue entered my lips tasting the sweetness from the desserts. A low groan rumbled in my throat as he drew me even closer to him. He grabbed me from behind and pulled me upwards, my legs locked around his waist. The burning sensation wouldn't and couldn't go away. I needed him to calm down; I needed to calm down, that's what we needed.

Chapter 12

"You are so beautiful I can't control myself," he whispered against my lips.

He brought his lips to mine; he began to kiss me like a mad man. With his hands on my hips he motioned my body down to the futon. His body covered me; his knee went between my legs. The simple gesture turned me on. He smelled and tasted so delicious it made me lightheaded with delight.

His kisses soothed me. His fingers traced slowly down my neck and around to my belly. His hand stopped beneath my shirt, his strong fingers began grazing the top of my jeans.

Drake pulled me on top as he rolled over, removing his shirt off in the process. Now I was on top of him--straddling him--I began removing my shirt with haste. After the useless thing dropped to the ground, I cupped his face and brought it to mine. Kissing him, I bit his lower lip, teasing him. I pulled away but he soon pulled me back into him. His hands came from nowhere and grabbed my hips, making me smile in victory. My hands slipped south and began unbuckling his jeans; before I knew it he'd done the same. Perfect. Slowly he began pulling them down, exposing my neon blue booty shorts.

I felt the hard bulge beginning to form between Drake's thighs. He wanted me. His desire was like a drug to me, with every deep and erotic kiss, it was hard for me to resist him.

He slanted his mouth over mine, his tongue, which was wanted and welcomed in my mouth, wandered around wrecking every unruffled nerve I had left. I shivered with pleasure as his lips grabbed and licked my lower lip. Oh where am I to get the strength to resist him any longer, when his mere touches drove me into unconsciousness? I moaned and wondered if he was this great with other women. I mentally slapped myself, who knew I was such a slut. But I wanted him so much it could be deadly.

"Tell me you have a condom," I groaned, the feeling was too great to be interrupted.

"Already done," he cooed in my ear. I looked down and gasped.

"Oh, umm r-right, "I stammered. Lucas wasn't that big.

"What's wrong," he ended up asking. My cheeks began to burn, and I knew why.

"N-Nothing,"

"Don't worry babe. I'll be your coach, and you can be my apprentice." his voice was low and steady. I looked up and smiled enthusiastically.

"Oh yeah, guide me." I scooted up until my breasts were in place for his tasting. His eyes filled with a deep and lustful hunger. His mouth pinched into a devilish grin.

"I'll guide you into places you never knew existed." He said. Slowly I unfastened my bra, letting the straps slide slowly down my arms. Drake's eyes resembling huge emeralds widened in anticipation. As soon as my bra was dropped to the floor I smirked at his expression.

"Look at what I've been missing," His head popped up and he began to lick his lips. Yummy, they looked even more inviting now than a minute ago.

He placed his hands on the small of my back and another between my shoulders. He pushed me forward slowly and gave my nipple a teasing lick. I gasped quietly, that little lick was enough to leave me wanting more.

"Why'd you stop?" I asked him, pissed off that he left me hanging on the edge.

"I didn't know how my little sex kitten was going to react," he grinned sensually and rubbed my hips.

"Do it before I change my--" I couldn't finish my threat; his lips came crushing to mine with need and urgency. His kiss came down to my neck, my unexposed shoulders and finally my breasts.

He gave suck like a hungry little baby. I wrapped my hands around his neck and grabbed a handful of his hair into my hands. I moaned at the effects of his mouth and tongue that surged through my body. My head rolled back, I bit my lip to avoid moaning.

I felt myself growing wetter and wetter, enough playing around, I needed him inside me. Drake seemed to have read my mind. He positioned me on his waist, with one swift motion he pulled off my shorts. He groaned and angled my body with his. I looked down and saw that his cock growing harder and bigger than a couple seconds ago. I felt myself growing more, and more conscious. But either way I knew Drake wasn't going to stop, and for that, I felt grateful.

"No second thoughts?" He asked, caressing my ass cheeks. I nodded confirming his longing desire and placed my hands behind his neck. With that his thickened manhood entered me at last.

Drake slid his manhood slowly in and out. I cried out in anger, he was taunting me. I dug my nails deep into his shoulders.

"Faster...harder," I growled in his ear, as I was biting his ear lobe in the process. He took a hold of my hips. Roughly he pulled me onto him. I bounced eagerly with his rhythm; a loud moan soon escaped my lips.

He shoved himself deeper and harder inside me, slamming me to him one last time as my orgasm reached its peak.

*

I lay on top of Drake--heaving--as he traced small circles on my back. My head rested on his chest, his heart was still pounding in my ears. My hands can now reach the floor. I grabbed my bra and shorts and slipped them on quickly, as I returned to lie back on his chest.

"You know what this reminds me of?" Drake asked randomly.

I laughed at his question, "And what's that?"

"That song, by Ray, shit, I forgot the name." He rubbed his chin in thought…

"You mean Sexy Can I," I giggled. His eyes lit up in amusement and nodded. A grin stretched across on his face.

"How'd you know? I would have thought a little girl like you wouldn't listen to that type of music," He teased me, causing me to blush. I slapped his arm softly and said…

"If I'm a little girl, then that makes you a pervert. Anyway, Sandra was the one who made me watch 'The Hangover' movie alright. Blame her." I quickly defended myself.

"You win," he answered. I nodded in agreement, as my eyelids began to close. I groaned in exhaustion and slept.

"One more thing, a friend of mine's coming over." Drake's voice sounded muffled. I let that information slip to the back of my mind and thoroughly enjoyed a peaceful slumber.

Chapter 13

I woke up feeling light-headed. I think maybe it was because of the heat, I didn't know. So I decided the best thing to do in this situation was take a long and cool shower. I sighed, yeah, that's exactly what I need. Now I woke up in the big comfy bed I had grown used to over the last couple of weeks. Drake was lying face down beside me. My eyes scanned the room for my clothes; as soon as I spotted them I got up from the bed and quietly walked across the room.

Clothes were scattered everywhere. I sighed in frustration, this wasn't getting me anywhere! I searched among the clothes around the room until I found my sweatpants.

"Calm down Kristen, you'll find your shirt," as I spoke to myself aloud.

"Is something wrong," he said. His voice still sounded tired as he spoke from behind me. I shifted my body around to see Drake walking towards me. A smile cleared on his tired face.

My face softened, he looked down-right adorable, but as tired as ever though.

"Oh nothing, I can't find my shirt that's all." I turned around and began shuffling through the clothing strewn across the floor. Drake's hands came from behind and wrapped themselves around my waist, and his chin was resting on my shoulder.

"You mean that one tank top?" He asked as he leaned against my ear. I turned around and nodded our faces a few inches apart.

"That's the one," I said enthusiastically. He slowly removed his hands from my waist, only to interweave them with my fingers.

"No, I haven't seen it," his eyes revealed that he was clearly hiding something. Nonetheless, my face dropped in disappointment. He placed his thumb on my chin and lifted my face until our eyes became locked on each other.

"On second thought, I did see a shirt like that around here, on the nightstand, Kristen." He smiled playfully. A yawn escaped those deliciously gorgeous lips.

"Thanks for the help. You look tired as hell though, maybe you should rest."

He nodded in agreement, then as quickly as he got up, he slammed himself back on the bed. I stood there for a while, watching Drake in his restful sleep.

What was wrong with me, I just had sex with this person, my fiancé from some prearranged deal of my mother's. I didn't know anything worthwhile about him; and what I did know wasn't anything you would feel comfortable knowing about your fiancé. For one thing, he had a reputation of being a womanizer. Another thing is that he is a wild party freak that was known for getting involved with tons of little rich girls. But besides all that I think he really does have feelings; and deep down there is a better person locked inside him waiting to come out.

When he talked about his Mother, there was sadness that was so genuine in his eyes that it made me want to do anything in my power to cure his wound. Hopefully that was not all an act, I thought to myself as I opened the bathroom door. As soon as my clothes were off, I turned the shower handle till the water was hot enough for my taste. My thoughts drained, just like the blazing hot water.

Drake's POV:

As I awakened with the sound of water bouncing from wall to wall from Kristen's shower, I sat up and looked around. From the looks of things, Kristen wasn't the tidiest person in the world. I wonder what was wrong with her this morning. She seemed somewhat unsteady this morning; a bit harder to understand than usual.

To tell the truth, I was ready for war yesterday. When I told her about my friend coming over she didn't say or do shit. She didn't go off like the firecracker she usually was. Then again, she did look somewhat weary yesterday.

I smiled at the thought of yesterday. Kristen surprised me; she wasn't as innocent as I thought her to be. That's what I liked best about her. One moment she was fuming with anger, the next she was glowing with gladness. She was like a librarian one moment, then a sexy wildcat the next.

She had so many sides to her. With every new discover, she always surprised me. So when she responded so well to the news, I had to raise an eyebrow.

My best friend Mark was scheduled to arrive today. His dad and mine were partners in crime back in the day. Or so they've told us. We practically grew up together, took our first steps together, and had our first words together. My mom, I remember didn't like that at all. Instead of saying 'Mommy' like most babies --my first word, believe it or not, was 'Fucker'. We were always around my dad and Mark's father Steve and their profane vocabulary was what we had to learn from.

My Dad was so proud; he laughed his ass off, well, until my mom silenced him with the death glare. I sighed heavily, those were the days. We were carefree...

Unlike our fathers Mark and I are the exact opposite. But there was always something that always made us get along. He liked eating healthy, while I preferred chips and chocolate bars. I was excellent with the ladies; he on the other hand was like I am around here with Kristen; a one woman man. He liked to study, while I would say 'fuck that, the games' on.' He was the goody, goody person; and I was the bad boy who wouldn't follow anyone's rules except for my own. Somehow, we kept each other in check.

I finally stood up and changed into some cargo shorts and a tee shirt. While I was at it I took the opportunity to clean up a bit around here. Kristen' shirts were scattered everywhere.
Wow, who knew somebody like Kristen would be this disorganized; surprise, surprise.

Maybe Mark could help me figure her out.

Kristen' POV:

Knock, knock.

Doesn't Dominic have a damn key? I finished putting on some short shorts, and makeup; now there. The walk to the door wasn't far, but I walked to the door slowly thinking that it was only Dominic. But to my surprise when I opened the door there stood this outrageously handsome male. He had honey brown hair just below his cars with a well fit body. He was wearing a plaid jacket and dark jeans. He was utterly breath-taking, but who the hell wears a jacket in this weather? This person I guess, and he was sexy as hell.

"'About time," I said standing there looking like a deer caught in the headlights. He looked away from his book and his dark butterscotch eyes widened quickly as he looked at me.

"Holy shit..., I...I'm sorry." He stammered. I had to smile at his awkward apology.

"Not to worry, its fine," I told him and smiled at him reassuringly. He smiled back,

"I'm Mark Parkour," He extended his hand, which I gladly shook.

"Kristen Whitmore, pleasure to meet you Mark." I mimicked him, adding my last name to the introduction.

"Likewise, Kristen is Drew here?" He asked still holding my hand. I must say, for a guy his hands were quite smooth.

"By Drew… I'm thinking… you mean Drake, right?" I asked just to be sure. He nodded in response and said…

"Yeah…"

"Come on in Mark," I turned around and began walking into the house, searching for Drake.

"Definitely," I heard Mark whisper. A smile tugged at the corners of my mouth for no apparent reason. I hope he was talking about his excitement to see Drake. Not the fact that I was walking in front of him with these short shorts.

"You must be the famous Kristen," He said out of nowhere. I stopped dead in my tracks and stared at him. My mom was big in the entrepreneur business, but not awfully big.

"What do you mean?" I asked. His eyes squinted with wonder; maybe he wasn't supposed to tell me. Well he's screwed now and needs spill those beans.

"Drake and Peter have been telling me about you. You're his fiancé, if I'm not mistaken. I have to tell you though; you're nothing like I imagined you." He said finally said.

My brows furrowed, "how did you imagine me?" I had to ask.

"For one, you don't act like the 'rich girl' stereotype. Second, you've been giving Drake a hard time. For that, you deserve a big ass round of applause." He looked at me and smiled. A jittery laugh escaped my lips. If he only knew that I'd actually given in to Drake and my desires.

"I don't consider myself as rich, just a normal person living a normal life. But, how would you know I've been giving him a hard time?" Come to think if it, why was Mark even here. I highly doubt he was here to leave some message or package for Drake. By the looks of his luggage he was here to stay.

Then it hit me. Drake said something last night about a friend coming over. Anger started to boil quickly inside me. This was hardly fair! If he could have friends over, then why couldn't I? What a bastard.

"We've been talking, I'm sure he told you, right." He sounded a bit unsure.

"It might've slipped my mind," I mumbled honestly, "talking? So you guys have been talking about me," I was interrupted by Drake's laugh from the bedroom. You have great timing there Drake.

"Well, well, well. If isn't Marcus Parkour. Who'd you have to kill to get away from that psycho mom of yours?"

"What's up, cunt. Thanks for the warm words of welcome, dipshit."

"Anytime, bro." he smiled as he pulled Mark into one of those one-arm hugs that men do nowadays. I sighed, boys will be boys. They hardly noticed me during their little reunion.

"Mark, this beautiful woman right here," Drake came and stood next to me, and placed his arm around my shoulder as he continued, "Is Kristen, my fiancée." He looked down at me and smiled warmly. I returned it and looked over at Mark.

"We already had a little introduction, and yeah, she's very beautiful. That's easy to understand." Not once did Mark's eyes drift away from my frame. All I did was blush. Damn it, this shouldn't be happening. Before I knew it, Drake's arm fell to my waist and wrapped itself securely around it. His green eyes didn't hold amusement or playfulness. They were cold and intimidating.

"Dude, it's like a hundred fucking degrees in here. I wouldn't want you to faint on me." He commanded. Mark smirked at Drake's change in mood and walked away, giving me one last smile as he entered the bedroom.

"Is something wrong? Did I miss something?" I asked completely dumbfounded. Drake shook his head.

"It's nothing, I'll be back." He said and while walking away. Great, just fucking great, I thought. Of course there are some secrets from their past, and I'm left in the dark.

Chapter 14

"So where am I going to sleep?" Mark asked as he finished unpacking his suitcase.

"You can sleep on the ground, Mark." Drake joked. Since I was in the kitchen preparing the one meal I could do well--a sandwich, I threw Drake a slice of sourdough bread, hitting him mistakenly in the face with a thud.

"Ouch," he rubbed jaw. He looked down, picked up the piece of bread, and took a bite.

"I never did like sourdough," he said to himself. I smiled internally making a mental note. Damn it, Kristen. Don't take notes! I told myself. I should be making a list of the things he doesn't like. Just to make him eat them all.

"You can take the futon." I offered confidently. There was only one bedroom in this house, and we couldn't all sleep in one bed. That would be absolutely weird. It's bad enough sharing the bed with one hot male; one more would make a crowd.

"That shit's uncomfortable," Drake butted in. I sighed angrily and threw him another piece of bread. Bingo! Another perfect hit. I smiled in content, I surprise myself every day.

"You know, you should try out for baseball or something. You have a strong arm, babe." Drake mumbled as he rubbed his jaw yet again.

"The only reason you think it's uncomfortable because you're huge, Drake." I scolded at him.

"You're saying I'm fat, Kristen?" He patted his heart as if to console it and smirked, "that comment will do wonders for my ego."

"Good, your ego could use a wakeup call. Aren't I right, Mark."

Mark laughed at our little scenario and nodded in my favor. "Sorry, bro. She's right." I giggled at Drake's expression, he's was probably thinking Mark was going to side with him. Ha! He was so predictable. When he recovered he flipped Mark off playfully.

Mark smirked mischievously and threw a cushion at Drake's mischievous smile. I gasped out in surprise and giggled at how he was caught off guard. Mark turned to me and wiggled his eyebrows. I blushed in return and started laughing even harder.

Drake stood, with an even bigger cushion in his hands. "That was a bad move, you made a big mistake now you motherfucker." His expression now screamed two words: 'Sweet Revenge.'

He threw the Frisbee-like pillow and hit Mark right on the neck, making him fall over a chair gasping for air. I shrieked in horror and ran to where Mark was sprawled on the floor. By the time I got to him, he was crouching and rubbing his neck that was red from where the pillow struck.

"Is that the best you can do, you son of a bitch?" He said jokingly, his voice became low and husky. Drake laughing at his comeback motioned him forward for the next attack.

"Whoa, whoa, whoa you do realize you hit him in the neck, don't you" I asked Drake, who apparently didn't care if he did or didn't knock the air out of his friend.

"We always play around like this, Kristen. We came close to cracking our skulls once before, no big deal." He shrugged. I stared at both of them with an incredulous expression. Cracking their skulls?! Who were these two men--no, no, no, they weren't men. Men actually have brains, well some of them. Who were these two boys?

"Fine, kill yourselves then." I couldn't give a damn. Humph, the problem was I actually did care.

"I'm sorry if we scared you there, Kristen." I heard Mark whisper sincerely behind me.

"I wasn't scared," I quickly defended myself. That came out too fast, it actually sounded fake… Damn.

Mark smiled at my lie and stepped forward to show me his neck. The red spot had cleared. Not fully convinced I took the liberty of touching his silky skin with my finger tips. Just in case there were any signs of mistreatment.

My fingers lingered against his skin; to be honest I really didn't want to remove them. Mark's dark butterscotch eyes softened as his eyes met my plain brown ones.

"Ahem, aren't you going to check mine?" Drake broke our little moment, my head turned automatically. I strolled slowly to where he was standing. Stopping just a few inches away from him, my arm stretched out to rub his firm jaw. He smiled and pulled me closer to him, his arm pressed into the small of my back.

"You can't see that well when you're that far away," He whispered. I closed my eyes and sighed, being this close to him causes my head to spin, especially when I'm touching his face, and oh so close to those wonderful lips. Calm your ass down Kristen, I told myself internally.

"You're both fine." I murmured silently and walked towards the kitchen to finish with my sandwich. The little house is now still, and nothing but the sound of rustling waves can be heard in the distance.

Drake's POV:

What was wrong with me? I saw her smiling at Mark and my anger began to boil in me. When she was touching him, fury began to rage deep in my soul. I didn't know what the hell was going on, and frankly, it was scaring the shit out of me. I wanted Kristen for myself, and was not interested in sharing.

Not once in my life have I ever considered Mark to be my competition. Maybe I underestimated him. Maybe Kristen likes good boy type, Could it be that she sees something in Mark that she doesn't see in me.

I sighed in frustration; this was all new to me. Unlike Kristen, girls came begging to date me. But after all, I have never dated someone like her. She is definitely somebody new in my repertoire. She keeps herself apart with dignity and pride. She's a feisty little dragon that's not afraid to bite. I rolled over to lie on my side. She was sleeping quietly next to me. Her features are relaxed and calm. Damn, she is just so beautiful. She had no idea how she was making me feel or even my growing feelings for her.

I reached out and slid my finger softly across her cheek. Her skin was as smooth as silk.

I gently pulled her waist gently and motioned for her to move closer to me. Her arms curled up in her chest as she snuggled close into my ribs. As she moved nearer to me warmth spread throughout my body. Sighing in contentment I easily fell asleep.

*

I began to hear mumbling from the living that awakened me. I groaned and turned over restlessly in the empty bed. Kristen wasn't here. I patted the vacant area and looked around. She was nowhere to be found. Damn, she's with Mark. And why the hell did that even bother me. He had nothing on me that I knew for sure.

I got off the bed quickly, turned to the bathroom and brushed my teeth with haste. I pulled on some jeans and a tee shirt briskly and I was out the door.

My assumptions were correct. Kristen was sitting down next to Mark who was smiling like there was no tomorrow. I walked past them and entered the kitchen without a single glance back. Why was I feeling like this, this feeling was slowly tearing me apart? She could be with anyone she likes; I don't own her. We were only engaged out of pure convenience. There are no feelings involved.

"Good morning, Drake." Kristen said rather bubbly. I looked at her skeptically and smiled doubtingly.

"You're Kristen, right."

She nodded smiling radiantly and smacked my arm slightly. Okay, something's wrong. Who was this person? Not that I was complaining.

"Oh shut up." She laughed.

"Hey I have an idea." I said quickly, both of them looked at each other and laughed. I scrunched my eyebrows letting them know I was getting mad. Why the hell would they be laughing?

"That's a first." Mark said between laughs. I laughed without humor and threw him a tablespoon. We would always be like this. Any other time I would not be concerned about what Mark had to say about me because we are always joking around with each another. But somehow, right now it bothered me terribly.

"Play nice, children," Kristen said as she held her hands up to stop.

"So do you want to know?" If they didn't than it was their loss.

"I do," she nodded enthusiastically. That's what I liked to see.

"Let's go to the docks. I don't want to be locked up anymore." I said calmly. Kristen smiled brilliantly, her eyes filled with that excitement and happiness that always filled me up inside.

"Let's go!" she agreed. I chuckled and nodded.

"But I'm allergic to the sun, remember." Mark blurted out. I smirked and turned around…

"Looks like you can't go then."

Chapter 15

"Really, in that case, we could just stay here if you like." I was feeling compelled to actually stay. I wouldn't mind either; Mark was a genuinely interesting person. He and Drake were practically raised together and yet they had nothing in common.

"I don't know," he said looking a bit unsure. While Drake looked impatient by his short and slow answers.

Drake said, "why not just you and I Kristen?" Drake grabbed my arm convincingly but I shrugged it off. Mark didn't say anything. Not even a single word. Drake's opinion didn't matter at this point.

"No you didn't, Drake," I turned to Mark and smiled, "do you want to come, we could think of something to help you; sunscreen maybe."

I didn't want to make him feel like the third wheel. That, I know, isn't the greatest feeling. To top it off, he has always been treated like Drake's shadow. Poor Mark, he was smart, funny, charming, handsome and kind. But he was always nothing more than a shadow when he stood next to Drake.

"Mark, we're going to be walking a lot. The suns' blazing and remember how you get those embarrassing rashes, not pretty, bro." Drake pressed the issue while pacing back and forth in impatience. What was up with both of them today? Or what was really going on with Drake? He's been acting weird ever since Mark arrived.

Mark lowered his head in disappointment, a faint blush cleared across his naturally tanned skin. "No need to bring that up. Yeah on second thought, I think I'll just stay around the house and relax. But, thanks for the offer, Kristen." He smiled reassuringly while Drake looked like a chubby little kid locked in a candy store. His smile couldn't possibly get any bigger.

"Are you sure? We could set up an umbrella to cover you on the boat. It's going to be boring here all alone."

Drake's smile was slowly disappearing. "No, I'm fine. I'll think of something to do around here, but thanks. Have fun." He smiled but I was still unconvinced.

"Fine, we will see you later." I waved. Drake pulled me into an embrace, leaving his arm on my waist and wrapping around me securely. He gently pulled me toward the door and out into the beautiful sun shine. We were far away and beyond Florida, but it was still the same sun. It's an absolute shame that Mark was allergic; he was missing out on so much. He told me that when he was little he didn't get to play much with the other kids. Drake was the only one that would stay behind and play checkers with him, over and over. The thought of a caring little Drake Montreal brought a smile to my face. I bet he was an extremely adorable kid.

His hands were no longer on my waist, so I decided to quickly walk out in front of him. Drake noticed my actions and began to do the same, walking along with equal haste. The sand on my feet gave me a feeling of serenity all over my body. The beach always has this effect on me, a special power that soothes all my problems away.

I looked over toward yacht and strangely enough it wasn't the same one I arrived on. Wow, they tired of the old one and purchased an even flashier one. How typical of the rich. We arrived at the dock and began to look over the new yacht. It was pale gray in color, and the windows were tinted and extremely shiny. All this for two people, I thought to myself.

As I approached the boat, and tried to board with my soaring 5'5" frame, I couldn't pull myself up on the boat. Ricky, the boatman who was probably in his fifties, well tanned and hairy--was glued to a magazine and had no intention of helping me anytime soon. Here comes Drake to my rescue, he gently grabbed me by the hips and lifted me up onto the deck of the yacht.

"Thanks," I murmured coolly. With one step Drake was already up on the boat. Damn his long legs.

"Anytime," he replied grinning like a fool. A hot fool, I'll give him that.

I took a seat on a lounger and sat quietly. I was a few seats down from Drake, which by the expression on his face was not the least bit pleased with the distance.

"Kristen, I don't bite." He said a bit loud so that I would be sure to hear. I was that far away that he had to speak louder than normal. But I had my reasons; he was acting like an ass today. What he did to Mark was monstrously unbelievable; I thought I would be unfair to him as well. He stood up and walked toward me, the yacht engine roared to life and began moving rapidly toward land.

Drake stopped when he was a few inches away from me and bent down. He placed his hand on my knee and began making swirls in a soothing manner. Oh God, please don't, it's already too hard to try to stay mad at him.

"Kristen, look at me." He whispered softly. Not a chance, I kept looking straight ahead. When I didn't look in his direction, he gently pulled my chin to turn my face toward him. His green eyes shimmered so magnificently, again I was breathless.

"If I did anything to piss you off, Kristen, I'm sorry. The last thing I want is for you to be upset with me no matter what the reason." I was surprised to say, it seemed as though he meant every single word of that apology. He soon cupped my face in his hands and pulled me into a much anticipated kiss. Drake's lips were much softer and kissable than the last time we kissed.

"Now c'mon, you can't see that well from this part of the boat." He took my hands and walked me to another lounging seat. This seat was much larger than the last and just the perfect place to view the sparkling ocean ahead.

I sat down, as far away from him as I could. He didn't like it one bit.

"Kristen, I won't bite unless you want me too." he smirked. I shook my head in disagreement and stayed where I was.

He took that as 'pull me to you, Drake' because that's what he did.

"Come here," he lightly pulled and seated me next to him. His hands slithered around my hips moving me closer to him. I gave in and cuddled with him, my head on his shoulder while his head was rested on mine.

"That's better," he whispered in my ear. I giggled and got up as fast as lightning, Drake's expression was a mix of things. I snickered at all of them.

"Now that I think about it, you might have rabies. Yuck." I was joking around, and started wiping my lips in pretend disgust. He stood slowly and smirked mischievously. He made his hands into adorable little claws and roared sensually.

"Well you better start running before I eat you for dinner, foxy." He said matter-of-factly and sniggered sexually. I couldn't help it but I snorted. Wow, Kristen, real smooth. I probably sounded like a pig. Since when did I care what he thought? The heat, yeah that's what it is, the heat.

"Wouldn't want that," I squealed tauntingly. Drake moved closer to me, slowly, just like a lion does to his pray. Okay, I'm seriously scared now. I started to dart across the deck trying to get as far away as possible from this crazy person behind me. It was like playing tag and when you have to get away from the person following you to the point that you even throw chairs to slow them down. That's what I was feeling at this point. I would move left and right avoiding objects.

Ricky at the wheel wasn't looking so happy either. As I passed him, I heard him grumble in his native language. His comment just went to the back of my mind as I ran to a compartment on the lower deck. Not until now did I realize Drake was really close to me. One more inch and he'd be tackling me. I cursed myself for not having longer legs.

"Kristen," He sang behind me. Damn, he sounds awfully close. I turned around for a glimpse and my assumptions were right. Screw me.

Strong arms closed in on me as we both fell onto a cushiony mattress. Great, we landed on a bed. I turned around to see Drake smiling in victory, his hands clasped around my head. I was trapped by his feet wrapped around my petite legs. Rape!

"Kristen, you're too slow. So much for that dream," He laughed.

"Ha, ha," I replied to his poor attempt of a joke.

"For that little stunt don't think you might owe me a little something?" He rubbed his chin in thought as he looked at me.

"How about a nice kick in the groin," I asked innocently. He shook his head and leaned in closely until the tips of our noses touched.

"You know what I want." He whispered a few inches away from my throbbing lips.

"This?" I raised my head a bit and our lips met in a taunting peck. I pulled away and smirked at his tortured expression.

"Kristen," he groaned, "more."

I listened to what he said and kissed him with as much force as I could put forward. His leg moved between mine demanding my acceptance. Drake's hand slid up and down the side of my stomach. Crap, I was screwed. I locked my arms around his neck roughly and brought him closer to me. I couldn't get enough.

Knock. Knock. Drake and I quickly stopped and looked up, both of us out of breath and heaving from our little make out session. Turns out it was our darling captain, Ricky. Never did like him.

"We're here" he grumbled, apparently he wasn't happy nor embarrassed that he interrupted us.

"Yeah, thanks a lot, Ricky." Drake said angrily. Ricky turned around and walked off snickering bitterly. Drake turned his attention to me and smiled apologetically.

"Sorry 'bout that. He's always the one to ruin everything." he got of the mattress and stood up lending me a hand. I took it and we walked outside; I didn't want Drake to see me blush. I didn't was him to see me blushing now. I could feel that I was blushing really hard, my face was literally burning.

"Watch out, Missy." Someone said gruffly behind me. I turned to see Ricky sitting comfortably in a wicker chair. The brim of his hat was sitting over his nose shading him from the sun.

"Y-yeah," I stammered pathetically. He laughed and shook his head but continued with his nap.

I sighed and walked to get my handbag. Tell me something I don't know, Ricky.

Chapter 16

She's been avoiding me. Every time I tried to talk to her she would only give me short answers and walk away 'pretending' to be surprised by something in the shops, yeah in the shops my ass. She's either pissed off or bothered by something, and that something has my name written all over it.

"Oh, look at that one!" She squealed randomly. I turned my head and looked at her in wonder. Those shorts she had on molded her ass perfectly. She had her hair loose, straight from the top and dropping down in soft curls. That tight top curved her body in the most appealing way that it was hard to look away. "Is it just me or did it get even hotter out here? It's probably me.

Kristen was all goo-goo-eyed over some turquoise bracelet. I just had to grin at her expression. Who knew a smile like that would really knock a guy out?

"How about it, my treat," I announced.

Kristen turned to me and frowned, "no, I'm not a gold digger, Drake. I have my own money."

I laughed out of pure amazement. I was offering a free bracelet and she turned it down. Something's going on in that head of hers. Jesus why do women have to be so complicated, especially this one?

"I wasn't trying to say that you were a gold digger. I'm simply offering you a bracelet, Kristen. No need to go all ninja on me." My hands came up to the side of my head in fake surrender. Her eyes turned to slits as she said…

"I'll go 'Ninja' on who ever I want," Kristen huffed, "and all I have to say is 'No, thank you very much.'" She turned around and entered the small shop. I sighed in defeat and followed.

I looked around the small room. Colorful beaded jewelry covers half the walls. A woman in her late forties stood behind the messy counter with a permanent scowl plastered on her face. I smiled politely but received no smile in return.

I turned to see Kristen having the hardest time trying to get the woman to understand her. She pointed to the bracelet in the display window and said each word slowly.

"That…one… I…Want…That…One…Please!" She pointed towards the piece that she wanted and smiled in anticipation, hoping that the woman understood her. The woman smirked and nodded her head in disagreement.

"Jaab Ijab mele le." The woman replied in Marshallese (no, I don't understand). Kristen's smile disappeared, she then came walking to me with a defeated pout and puppy-dog eyes.

"Help," she squeaked. I looked at her and smiled, but all of a sudden the woman started to laugh like she heard the funniest joke ever. My forehead creased as I stared at her,

"I was just kidding. I know the language, but so funny the face." She said between laughs. By funny face, I knew she meant Kristen's disappointment.

"Let's go, Kristen." I grabbed her arm gently and started to walk away. Someone like Kristen shouldn't be joked around with. She in one of the kindest people I knew, and that meant something. She deserved better than to be laughed at.

"I was only kidding! Here, comeback!" I heard the woman yelling from behind. Fuck that, we weren't going back there.

"Drake, what the hell was that? Oh, she was just having a little fun and by the looks of her face she doesn't get much of it." Kristen mumbled behind me and shrugged my hold off. I turned to look at her and was surprised when her features weren't angry, but rather soft and understanding.

"You're right. I seriously don't know why I flipped out like that. I guess I didn't like the way she was treating you." I said truthfully. She smiled and placed her soft hand on my cheek.

"Thanks for sticking up for me, Drake. I would have done the s--uh, I'm hungry. Sh-shall we go and have something to eat?" She added quickly. I knew that she had something more to say. So I pressed…

"That's not what you were going to say. You would've done the same for me?" I smirked, a bit surprised. She glared at me but only nodded, a faint blush rising from her cheeks.

"Morals, what can you do." She shrugged like it was nothing. I knew better.

"Either way you would've done the same thing, and not just because of your 'morals'," I smirked.

She snickered, "don't flatter yourself, Drake."

I seriously couldn't win with her.

"Fine, if that's what you want to believe. Now about that food, I'm hungry too." I looked around to see if there were any food courts nearby. Kristen shook her head and said…

"Why waste money. Can't we just call Dominic or Ricky to come and bring food that we're familiar with?" She suggested.

The fact was I didn't want to go home. I wanted more time alone with Kristen, without Mark in the middle of it all. Every time I think of Mark now, I am reminded of him and Kristen sitting together on the futon. To be honest, I didn't know what the hell was going on these days; mentally, physically or emotionally.

Mark was the brother I never had; he was not my enemy.

"That's okay with me." I finally gave in. She smiled cheeky and walked quickly next to me. Out of nowhere she took my hand into hers and examined it closely.

"You have soft hands, Drake. I never noticed." She said looking down at his hands. I laughed at how late she catches on to things.

"Runs in the family I guess…"

"Lucky you," She turned on her heals and began walking, letting his hand go in the process. Somehow, it just felt somewhat strange. Having her hand in mine felt wonderful; warmth spread throughout my body when she touched me, and now, not having her hand in mine just felt wrong.

"Who said you could let go?" I asked.

"What are you talking about?"

"This," I snatched one of her hands and ran my fingers between hers until they locked together perfectly. She blushed but nodded in response.

"I'm fucking hungry. Shall we eat?" I pulled her close to me and wrapped my arms around her petite waist. Kristen nodded in agreement.

"We shall." She responded eagerly.

I took out my phone and dialed Dominic's number; I figured Ricky would be too much of a distraction. I certainly wouldn't want our last encounter to repeat again.

"Hello, Mr. Montreal. How may I be of assistance?" Dominic said with his usual promptness and a clear and heavily accented voice.

"We need the yacht to get back. We have decided we're going to eat back at the house, so when you come to pick us up please bring us some food with you." I said professionally, my dad taught me that. If you want to establish a respectful relationship with your employees you have to act, dress, and talk professionally. Carry yourself with confidence and just enough self pride for respect. Not over doing it, then people will believe one thing and one thing only: You're a complete dick, simple as that.

"Of course, Mr. Montreal, I'll send Ricky right away--"

I cut him off before he could continue, "No Dominic, I want you specifically."

"Did something happen, Sir?" He ended up asking. God, why did they have to ask so many questions?

"Just send anyone but him." I said one last time before clicking the phone off on him. Rather rude, but at this point, who gives a shit.

"Calm down, Tiger. That wasn't very nice." Kristen pointed her index finger as if to say 'shame on me.'

"Hopefully he got the message." I muttered. She sighed and kept on walking, dodging anyone who walked in front of her with polite excuse me's.

Silence fell upon us, only the buzz of the market kept me sane. "Kristen, can I ask you something," I asked, this question's been bugging me for a while now, might as well spit it out now, "but you have to be honest, alright."

She nodded in response, "I'll play what you want to ask me?"

I sighed and looked up at the sky. How do I put this? "What do you think of Mark," I blurted out. She sighed in relief and smiled...

"Hmmm, what do I think of him." She tapped her chin and grinned, "I have no idea."

I looked at her seriously. That wasn't an answer. "Kristen, I'm being serious."

She looked at me and her grin disappeared, "He seems like a nice person, Drake. What more do you want me to say?"

Kristen didn't understand, did she? This wasn't a question on whether or not she thought he'd be the perfect best friend. She knows that this isn't fucking case; she's just avoiding the damn question.

"That wasn't my question, so answer it properly."

"Fine, I don't like him, Drake. If that's what you wanted to hear, then there it is." She said. By the change in her voice, I knew she was mad.

"Why are you mad, Kristen? If what you said is true, then you wouldn't have taken it so badly." I found myself saying, matching her anger. Not after I saw the look on Kristen' face did I realize what I had said.

"If you don't believe me, then fine. Believe any fucking thing you want." Kristen pulled her hand away from mine abruptly and began walking away as fast as she could.

I stood there, watching my surroundings disappear as I saw her walk away. Feeling like shit and a total dumbass I began walking numbly towards her. Why did she have to be so complicated?

Chapter 17

No, no, no, that went all wrong. Why did I freak out when Drake asked me that question? I mean, not that it was actually true. I did like Mark, but not in a romantic way. To be honest, I have no idea why I snapped like that. A few seconds later, I realized how much I probably hurt Drake. I just didn't want to apologize, thinking he would've yelled right in my face.

I walked and walked steadily until I reached the yacht. A young man in his mid twenties appeared on the surface of the boat. He smiled happily at our arrival and extended his hand to assist us—or rather to help me. Drake and his long legs didn't need help.

"You must be Kristen Whitmore; it's a pleasure to meet you." He smiled politely. I returned the smile,

"The pleasure's all mine, uh…" I paused and squinted my eyes, he got the message and replied,

"Dominic, Ms. Whitmore."

"Nice to finally meet you Dominic," I smiled and walked onto the yacht.

"She a keeper, Mr. Montreal," I heard Dominic whisper to Drake, assuming that I wouldn't hear. Dominic just has a naturally loud voice.

"Yeah," I heard Andrew reply back. The strange thing was that I could literally feel him smiling. Perfect, the guilt that was piled up inside me grew heavier to the point where I couldn't take it anymore.

"Uh, Drake, Can I talk to you?" I asked timidly. Maybe he was still upset with me; even I knew I acted like a total bitch back there.

"Uh yeah sure," He said a bit unsure himself.

He walked up to me while Dominic walked in the opposite direction. "What's up?" He had stopped a few feet away from me. I rolled my eyes and slowly looked up at him, erasing the space between us. He knew what was coming and smiled brightly. Beneath the smile there was a feeling of relief.

"Look, I'm sorry I acted like a moody bitch back there. It was just a question and you were right. I don't have romantic feelings for him, so that was completely uncalled for." My hands glided up his torso until I reached his firm chest. I looked up at him with the biggest puppy-dog eyes I could make, and said ever so softly, "I'm sorry."

Drake smirked and nodded. "You're forgiven, although I do ask for something in return." He said with a devilish smirk playing around those juicy lips.

"And what might that be?" I asked innocently. He didn't say a word; all he did was bend his head in my direction and placing a firm kiss right on my chapped lips. He seemed to notice this and licked them. I wanted to burst out laughing, that was unbearably ticklish. Drake grinned and touched the tip of my nose with his index finger.

"Who knew you would be ticklish, especially on the lips." He laughed while his hands stayed and caressed my hips. Consolation shot throughout my body. No matter how hard I tried, I could never stay mad at him.

"Mr. Montreal sir, Uh, no intention of interrupting, but your father would like to speak to you." Dominic blurted out hesitantly. Drake nodded,

"Be there in a second, Dominic." By the sound of his voice he wasn't all too happy. Drake looked at me with an apologetic expression and said, "That's twice now. I'll be back." He kissed me gently on the forehead and walked away to the captain's compartment.

Dominic walked outside while Drake closed the door behind him. He sat on the nearest wicker chair and hunched his shoulders in exhaustion. Suddenly I felt sympathy for the poor guy. He was a few years older than me, and probably didn't have a social life.

"Are you okay, Dominic?" I had to ask. He immediately shot up and began looking around anxiously,

"Is there something you need, Ms. Whitmore? Anything I could get for you?" His facial features all screamed the words 'Tired as hell, so fuck off.'

"I was going to ask if, um… you had a…phone I could um… borrow," I said quickly. Maybe awakening him wasn't the best idea. He yawned and plastered a tired smile on his face.

"Follow me, Ms. Whitmore." He hid his exhaustion very well. Guess he was used to it by now.

"Call me Kristen. You're making me feel old." I chuckled. He laughed lightly and nodded.

"Fine, Ms. Mad-- I mean, Kristen."

Dominic ended up taking me to a small compartment with a small bed. There was a night stand beside the bed, and on the night stand was a phone. This will definitely do.

"Thanks." I said. He nodded and walked off without another word. I jumped on the bed and took the phone into my hands, my fingers automatically dialing Sandra's number. She picked up on the fourth ring sounding very irritated.

"I don't want to buy your damn cookies! So do me a favor and leave me the fuck alone, Jenny! If you don't stop, I swear on my dead rabbit's grave I will tell everyone about the day you got the shits and messed up your pants!" Whew, she's really irritated.

I giggled loudly and said, "Jenny shitted her pants! Holy crap, who would've…"

She gasped in horror, "I-I-I no... That's not what I meant! I meant…whoa, whoa, whoa. Kris, is that you?" She suddenly came to the realization and sighed in relief.

"Yup, long time no talk." I laughed. God, I missed this wild goose.

"Kristen, you bitch!" She screamed into the phone rather closely. Wow, this is what I get from my 'Best friend'. I missed her.

"Umm, thanks? You warm my heart with your kind words, Sandra." I sobbed dramatically.

"You left me hanging for about...one...two...three...five... weeks! I didn't have a number, no nothing!" Sandra bellowed.

"5 Weeks? It's seems less than that." I muttered more to myself than anything.

"Yeah five weeks, whoa, wait a minute there...you know what they say, time flies when you're busy." She said. From this end of the line you could tell she was excited. And if I knew Sandra, a wicked smile was slowly forming at her lips right about now.

"Isn't it, 'Time flies when you're having fun'?" I asked, trying to avoid the questions she was about to bombard me with any second now.

"Bitch, I know what you're doing, so quit it. Spill! Did you make-out? French, peck? I need to know this! Holy shit, you had sex didn't you? Holy fucking shit, you had sex! How was he? Below average, average, above average, or advanced. Oh my god, how big? Kristen, you're not answering!

Classic Sandra, "Breath, and if you want me to answer then you're going to have to slow it down." I said simply, playing with the phone cord as I tried hard not to laugh. If I did, it would be heard a mile away.

"Fine, so tell me unless you want me to die here on the spot."

"Nope, here it is. We did have sex. We did make-out. Quite a few times actually. Advanced, and umm, pretty big, Sandra." I blushed at the memory.

The phone was about 5 feet away from my ear, Sandra's piercing screams made my right ear throb. I had to crack a smile, mention the word 'sex' and she'll be there. "Oh. My. God! I knew it. Didn't I tell you something was going to go down? Didn't I tell you? Man, I am so good." Sandra screamed out laughing. She'd be shaking my shoulders right about now out of pure excitement.

"Yeah, yeah, yeah, so you did, oh wise Sandra." My fingers tangled the phone cord as I sighed.

"So, are you guys together?" She asked enthusiastically.

"I--think--maybe--I have no idea." I told her honestly. Over the past weeks I knew my feelings towards him changed. He wasn't the obnoxious player but rather, a nice and caring person I knew was somewhere beneath that mask. He was still a goofy guy who managed to make me smile and laugh without a care in the world. Being near him and his wonderful aura intoxicated me, causing my thoughts and worries to disappear. Just like some drug or hard liquor. Something I couldn't live without.

"You amaze me, Kristen. You're so oblivious to other people's feelings." How true, but what could I do about it.

"Okay, okay. I get you, Sandra. Guess what."

"Ooh, I like where this is going. Enlighten me." The excitement never wears off.

"He brought a friend over."

"A friend, huh, is he cute? Is he my type? If he isn't then I'll die. It's not fair; you get to be on a private island with two hot guys. What did I do to deserve this? Boo--who--who." She wailed dramatically. At this point it was hard to resist laughing, so I literally popped in a few of giggles.

"His name is Mark and well, I guess you can say he's hot. But I doubt he's your type." I said to her casually. Sandra always liked her guys with an edge. She likes the bad boys who always break the rules. Mark was everything but a rebel.

"And who are you to say he is or isn't my type? He sounds hot already. Well I can't wait to feast my eyes on that beauty, I trust you to tell me the truth, Kris. If he's ugly, well, let's just say Jigsaw's waiting for you when you get back, so no pressure." She finished off brightly. I can't wait to get home.

"Not like it hasn't been a pleasure talking to you, Sandra but I have to go. I swear that I'll call you as soon as I can. Yes, I will tell you all the juicy details. Love you."

"Ha, ha, real funny, Oh Kristen, you know me so well. Alright then, talk to you soon. Love you."

The line went dead. How much I missed that girl. I hate to admit it but I also miss my crazy mother. I'll be thanking her for the condoms. She really saved my ass with that one.

I hung up the phone and began walked back toward the main deck. Dominic was no longer resting. I assumed he was talking with Drake and Peter, either that or in the bathroom. Each one was probable. I strolled towards the far end of the yacht and looked out to sea. The sun still high on the sky made the ocean sparkle beautifully. Salty air hit me in all directions, making my hair dance. I closed my eyes and fully enjoyed the moment, with nothing more than the calming sea around me.

I know I probably looked stupid but I couldn't help myself. I spread my arms like a soaring eagle and smiled at the feeling it created.

A few seconds later those familiar arms began to caress my waist and then entangled themselves with my own arms, mimicking my movements.

"I'll be your Jack if you be my Rose." Drake murmured against my neck.

I smiled at the thought, and nodded slowly. He kissed me softly at the nape of my neck.

"Sounds great to me" I turned to face him and planted a soft kiss on his lips.

He smiled against my lips, and settled his forehead on top of mine. "We should be going, I'm starving."

"Is that all you think about is Food?" I shook my head laughing. Drake nodded and looked out at Marjorie Island. The sun was gradually setting over the horizon and the breeze that came along with it sent chills throughout my body.

"Bye, Dominic."

"Good Bye, Kristen." His voice did sound he was thoroughly beat.

"You should get some rest, Dominic." I decided to tell him. He nodded and smiled warmly,

"Planning on it madam, good bye." He finished off with a yawn. Drake looked at us both with an amused expression. He grinned and walked over to the little house I have come called home for the past five weeks. A groan escaped my lips when I noticed that my feet were killing me.

Drake seemed to notice my whining because he came running over to me. "What's wrong?"

I shook my head and looked down. My feet were throbbing, "My feet, but it's nothing. I'll live, let me by." I pushed him aside and began walking.

"No, you're not. Here, get on top." Drake bent down and patted his back, motioning me to hop on his back.

"Oh, can I get a piggy-back ride!" I asked. He nodded and bent down even lower. Drake's expression was something that couldn't be denied. I laughed and sauntered to him. My legs eagerly wrapped around his well defined back and locked themselves beneath him. He stood up unhurriedly and grasped my legs for balance.

With his strength and long legs we arrived in no time. Once we got to the porch he put me down and opened the door. The lights were off in the drawing room as well in the kitchen. There was no Mark here or there. As we proceeded further into the house we spotted him sprawled on the couch in nothing but a pair of boxers on. Don't stare, don't stare.

"Umm, should we wake him?" I couldn't help but ask. It was only about three or four in the evening, and here I thought I was the heavy sleeper.

"It's your choice."

Chapter 18

I didn't want to seem rude, so I did what seemed best and woke him up. Drake nodded and smiled then walked casually to the kitchen.

Mark was still on the futon looking like he was having the time of his life sleeping. God, I didn't want to ruin it. I sighed and knelt before him. His back was bare, as well as every other inch of his body—except that down below.

I studied him closely. He was tanned even though he was allergic to the sun. Unlike Drake, Mark's back was less muscular but it still well managed to look appealing. No, it wasn't because he wasn't fit; he's just not as muscular.

"Mark, wake up." I began to say softly.

"Mark, if you want to eat you must get up." I said a bit more annoyed. My feeble calls didn't do much.

"Mark!" I began shoving harshly.

A small laugh came from the kitchen. I turned and saw Drake leaning in the doorframe looking very amused. "That's what both of you have in common. The heaviest sleepers I have ever known." He shook his head and laughed.

"How could you possibly know I'm a heavy sleeper?" I challenged. He looked at me like I said the stupidest thing in the world.

"Kristen, you and I share a bed. I've been sleeping next to you for the last couple of weeks." He grinned, "The best nights of my life."

I blushed at what he said and stood up, forgetting about Mark at one point. "Humph, I had better." I teased.

He looked hurt for a few seconds, but after he saw the smirk on my face his facial features turned seductive. "For a minute there I thought you actually meant what he said. Now we all know you're lying." He snickered.

I pushed him up against the wall, running my hands up his torso. "Whatever helps you sleep at night, Drew?" I whispered sensually.

"Touché, babe" Drake murmured against my cheek, setting butterfly kisses as he went up to my awaiting lips. The feeling of having his mouth moving in sync with mine was already missed. It's been almost twenty minutes since our mouths intertwined. They needed interplay, and my lips were already throbbing for interaction.

As we were mere inches away from kissing Mark's voice rang around the small house. "Kristen, Drake."

I opened my eyes to stare at Drake's annoyed expression. He turns around and said, "Nice going, bro. You always had the greatest timing."

I giggled and walked around Drake, whose fumes were deadly clear. "Food's on the table, Mark." I smile, but my gaze soon falls down south. He sees my eyes trail down and automatically blushes deep crimson. He smiled sheepishly,

"I'm sorry; I thought you'd be out longer." He stood up quickly and cupped his manhood into his hands.

Drake smirked, "C'mon, Mark. It's not like you have anything to hide."

I bit my lip to keep myself from laughing. Mark's faced turned a deeper shade of red and he then literally ran out of the room. Drake laughed victoriously and looked at me,

"Don't tell me you didn't find that funny."

I walked up to him and smacked his arm cordially, "No," I lied, "now go over there and say you're sorry."

Drake raised his brow at me and mused, "I don't think I will." He teased.

"Please," I pouted.

Drake sighed and nodded, "Fine, but I want those lips later."

I laughed and watched him walk away, admiring his ass while I was at it.

*

A few minutes went by until both Drake and Mark—fully dressed—came out laughing like the world depended on it. They both look so giddy it warmed my heart. Drake had his arm wrapped around Mark's shoulders in a manly way while he messed up his already tousled hair.

"You two look happy," I inquired.

Drake nodded and walked up to me until his arms were securely around my waist, "Shall we eat."

"We shall," Mark and I said simultaneously. We looked at each other and laughed softly. Drake glided me towards the kitchen. He pulled out one of the stools and patted the seat, motioning me to have a seat.

Drake walked around the island and started setting plates here and there. He got ingredients out of a small container and poured it onto a pan, placing a chicken breast on top of the condiments. My eyes flickered around his moving body; every single inch of his being was perfect in every way. I stared at him in awe until Mark snapped me out of my trance.

"Don't add parsley," He told Drake over a small vase that was blocking his view.

"Oh, right. You're allergic." He snorted. I turned to Mark, pretty sure I was gawking.

"How many things are you allergic to?" I couldn't help the smile forming around my mouth.

He shrugged like it was no big deal and said, "A few things."

The way he said it clearly stated that he didn't want to keep talking about the subject, too bad Drake was already answering me, "Pineapples, artificial flavors, peanuts, parsley, and of course, the sun." He said it like it was tattooed on the palm of his hands. What surprised me wasn't the fact that Mark was allergic to quite a few things, but what did was the fact that Drake knew it so well.

"Allergies are nothing reason for shame." I assured Mark.

He laughed along with Drake who was now laughing, "I'm not ashamed, I just don't think it's that big of a deal."

"Oh," was all I could say.

Drake looked at me adoringly over his shoulder and said, "Are you allergic to anything, Kris? I wouldn't want to accidently poison you."

"Not that I know of," I laughed.

He nodded and turned his attention back to the food. After a few minutes, Drake finally finished with our dinner. He picked up the small chicken breast with a spatula and placed it very gently onto my plate. The expression he wore was downright hilarious. It was like the chicken breast was this newborn child.

"Hey, you can never be too careful; not even with food." He winked for no apparent reason. I giggled and began cutting my food with a knife. Drake came around and sat next to me.

"This isn't bad, Andy boy, not bad." Mark nodded in satisfaction beside me.

"How many nicknames do you have, Drake." I asked curiously.

He looked over at me and wrinkled his nose in the most adorable way possible. "Not many. Andy and Drew are it. Of course, Drake is for the ladies." He wiggled his eyebrows and smirked. I nudged him on the ribs and shook my head smiling.

"You surprise me with your confidence, Drake."

"Likewise," He smiled with a mouth full of food. My stomach rumbled below me and I decided it was time to finally eat.

*

Once we were all done, we took up our plates and put them in the sink. The minute the two guys left the kitchen without cleaning up their mess; I stomped up to them and pulled them back by their collars.

"Clean up time, boys." I smirked at the horrified expression the two gave me.

"Don't whine like little girls. Now, Drake you have dish duty. Mark, you can take out the garbage." I pointed at the stations they were about to clean up. They began working, muttering the words 'bossy' or 'clean-freak' occasionally.

I went around and made sure they were doing things right. Drake was smacking the dishes with the sponge to get the blob of dried grease cleaned out; which wasn't doing any good.

I bit my lip to keep me from giggling. He looked so oblivious to what he was doing. I felt bad laughing at his misery." Uh Drake, you're doing it wrong."

He looked at me with his brows scrunched together. "Would you mind helping me?"

"Nope, do it yourself." I laughed.

He sighed impatiently and grumbled, "You're evil." He said under his breath.

I shrugged and looked around. Mark was nowhere to be seen. I turned to Drake and said, "Where's Mark?"

"He—he--he is outside."

I turned my heels and slid the back door opened. As soon as I did, fresh air whipped all around me. Since I was only wearing some denim shorts and a tank-top, all I could do was shiver. My head looked sideways, from right to left. I walked under the porch light and it lit up automatically. With more light surrounding me I looked both ways again.

I hugged myself even tighter as I walked further outside. "Mark?"

The wind was my only response. My feet dragged me deeper outdoors. While I was walking along side the house I heard a loud bang that made me jump. Trying to keep my heart from running away from my chest I walked around the house's corner.

Mark was trying to put the whole garbage bag inside the garbage can. I giggled internally; the way he was standing was very amusing.

"Need some help?" I asked timidly.

He stared at me for what seemed like forever and finally nodded. "Something inside poked me. Since there isn't any light here it's hard to notice where the spike came from."

"Okay, so what do you want me to do? Do I hold it from here...or here?"

"Anywhere's fine. Just be careful." He warned me, making me roll my eyes.

"I'm always careful."

The black bag was now a bit above my shoulder. Mark pulled it up and ordered me to grab it from the bottom. My hand went under the surprisingly heavy bag, but as soon as this happened I ended up poking myself with something fairly sharp.

"Ouch," I quickly let go of the bag and rubbed my fingers together.

"Yeah, you're always careful." Mark said sarcastically.

I pouted "That really hurt."

"Told you," He came up to me and took my hand in his. Placing his hand gently on my bleeding finger he dabbed it with a clean napkin.

"There you go." His face was inches from mine. He seemed to realize and leaned in closer.

I knew where this was going and I couldn't let it happen, "Mark, stop." Just like my feeble calls a few minutes ago he ignored them completely. Instead of backing up he leaned in even closer. He pulled my face to his with his thumb on my quivering chin. "W-what are you doing, Stop."

It was too late.

Chapter 19

I didn't want to seem rude, so I did what seemed best and woke him up. Drake nodded and smiled then walked casually to the kitchen.

Mark was still on the futon looking like he was having the time of his life sleeping. God, I didn't want to ruin it. I sighed and knelt before him. His back was bare, as well as the rest of him—except that region below.

I studied him closely. He was tanned even though he was allergic to the sun. Unlike Drake, Mark's back was less muscular but it still managed to look appealing. He was not as muscular

"Mark, wake up." I began softly.

No response.

"Mark, if you want to eat you must get up." I said a bit more annoyed. My feeble attempts didn't accomplish much.

"Mark!" I began shoving harshly.

A small laugh came from the kitchen. I turned around to see Drake leaning on the doorframe looking very amused. "That's what both of you have in common. The heaviest sleepers I've know." He shook his head and laughed.

"How could you possibly know I'm a heavy sleeper?" I challenged. He looked at me like I said the stupidest thing in the world.

"Kristen, you and I share a bed. I've been sleeping next to you for the past weeks." He smiled, "those nights have been the best nights of my life."

I blushed at what he said and stood up, forgetting about Mark at one point. "Humph, I had better..." I teased.

He looked hurt for a few seconds, but after he saw the smirk on my face his facial features turned seductive. "For a minute there I thought you actually meant that. Now we all know you're lying." He snickered.

I pushed him up against the wall, running my hands up his torso. "Whatever helps you sleep at night, Drew," I whispered sensually.

"Touché, babe," Drake murmured against my cheek, sending butterfly kisses as he came close to my eager lips. The feeling of having his mouth moving in sync with mine was already missed. It's been almost twenty minutes since our mouths intertwined. They needed interplay, and my lips were already throbbing for interaction.

As we were mere inches away from kissing Mark's voice rang around the small house. "Kristen, Drake?"

I opened my eyes to notice Drake's annoyed expression. He turned around and said, "Nice going, bro. You always had the greatest timing."

I giggled and walked around Drake, whose fumes were deadly clear. "Food's on the table, Mark." I smiled, but my gaze soon fell south. He sees my eyes falling downward and automatically he blushes to a deep crimson. He smiled sheepishly,

"Ooh I'm sorry; I thought you'd be out longer." He stood up quickly and cupped his manhood into his hands.

Drake smirked, "C'mon, Mark. It's not like you have anything to hide."

I bit my lip to keep myself from laughing. Mark began to blush a deeper shade of red and literally ran out of the room. Drake laughed victoriously and looked at me,

"Don't tell me you didn't find that funny."

I walked up to him and smacked his arm cordially, "No," I lied, "now go over there and say apologize."

Drake raised his brow at me in amusement, "I don't think I will." He taunted.

"Please," I pouted.

Drake sighed and nodded, "Fine, but I still want those lips."

I laughed and saw him walk away, admiring his ass while I was at it.

*

A few minutes went by until both Drake and Mark—fully dressed—came out laughing like the world depended on it. They both look so giddy together it warmed my heart. Drake had his arm wrapped around Mark's shoulders in a manly way while he messed up his already tousled hair.

"You two look happy," I inquired.

Drake nodded and walked up toward me until his arms were securely around my waist, "Shall we eat?"

"We shall," Mark and I said simultaneously. We looked at each other and laughed softly. Drake glided me towards the kitchen. He pulled out one of the stools and patted the seat, motioning me to be seated.

Drake walked around the island and started setting plates here and there. He got ingredients out of a small container and poured it onto a pan, placing a chicken breast on top of the condiments. My eyes flickered around his moving body; every single inch of his being was perfectly in sync. I stared at him in awe until Mark snapped me out of my trance.

"Don't add parsley," He told Drake over a small vase that was blocking his view.

"Oh, right. You're allergic." He snorted. I turned to Mark, pretty sure I was gawking.

"How many things are you allergic to?" I couldn't help the smile forming around my mouth.

He shrugged like it was no big deal and said, "A few things."

The way he said it clearly gave the impression that he didn't want to continue on about the subject, too bad Drake was already answering me, "Pineapples, artificial flavors, peanuts, parsley, and of course, the sun." He said it like it was tattooed on the palm of his hands. What surprised me the most wasn't the fact that Mark was allergic to quite a few things, but that Drake knew them so well.

"Allergies are nothing to be ashamed of." I assured Mark.

He laughed along with Drake now also laughing, "I'm not ashamed, I just don't think it's that big of a deal."

"Oh," was all I could say.

Drake looked at me adoringly over his shoulder and said, "Are you allergic to anything, Kris? I wouldn't want to accidently poison you."

"Not that I know of," I laughed.

He nodded and turned his attention back to the food. After a few minutes, Drake finally finished with our dinner. He picked up the small chicken breast with a spatula and placed it very gently onto my plate. The expression he wore was downright hilarious. It was like the chicken breast was this newborn child.

"Hey, you can never be too careful, even with food." He winked for no apparent reason. I giggled and began slicing my chicken with a knife. Drake came around and sat next to me.

"This isn't bad, Andy boy, not bad at all." Mark nodded in satisfaction beside me.

"How many nicknames do you have, Drake." I asked curiously.

He looked over at me and wrinkled his nose in the most adorable way possible. "Not many. Just Andy and Drew is all. Of course, Drake is for the ladies." He wiggled his eyebrows and smirked. I nudged him in the ribs and shook my head smiling.

"You surprise me with your confidence, Drake."

"Likewise," He smiled with a mouth full of food. My stomach was growling below me and I realized it was really time to finally eat.

*

Once we were all done, we took up our plates and put them in the sink. At the very same minute the two guys tore from the kitchen without cleaning up their messes. I stomped up right behind them and pulled them back into the kitchen by their collars.

"Clean up time, boys." I smirked at the horrified expression the two gave me.

"Don't whine like little girls. Now, Drake you have dish duty, and Mark, you have the garbage." I pointed at the stations they were about to clean up. They began working, muttering the words 'bossy' or 'clean-freak' occasionally.

I went around to make sure they were doing things right. Drake was smacking the dishes with the sponge to get the blob of dried grease cleaned; which wasn't doing any good.

I bit my lip to keep me laughing. He appeared so oblivious to what he was doing that I really felt bad laughing at him. "Uh, Drake, you're doing it all wrong."

He looked at me with his brows scrunched together. "Would you mind helping me?"

"Nope, do it yourself." I laughed.

He sighed impatiently and grumbled, "You're evil," he said under his breath.

I shrugged and looked around. Mark was nowhere to be seen. I turned to Drake and said, "Where's Mark?"

"He's outside."

I turned my heels and slid the back door open. As soon as I did, fresh air began to circle around me. Since I was only wearing some denim shorts and a tank-top, all I did was shiver. My head looked sideways, from right to left. I walked under the porch light and it lit up automatically. With more light surrounding me I looked both ways once more.

I hugged myself even tighter as I walked further outside. "Mark?"

The wind was my only response. My feet kept moving toward the ever so inviting outdoors. While I was walking around the side the house I heard a loud bang that made me jump. Trying to keep my heart from leaping from chest I walked around the house's corner.

Mark was trying to put the whole garbage bag inside the garbage can. I giggled internally; the way he was standing was very amusing.

"Need some help?" I asked timidly.

He stared at me for what seemed like forever and finally nodded. "Something from inside poked me. Since there isn't any light out here it's hard to tell what was poking me."

"Okay, so what do you want me to do? Do I hold it from here, or here?"

"Anywhere is fine. Just be careful." He warned me, making me roll my eyes.

"I'm always careful."

The black bag was now a bit above my shoulder. Mark pulled it up and ordered me to grab it from the bottom. My hand went under the surprisingly heavy bag, but as soon as this happened I ended up poking myself with something fairly sharp again.

"Ouch." I quickly let go of the bag and rubbed my fingers together.

"Yeah, you're always careful." Mark told me sarcastically.

I pouted "That really hurt."

"Told you," He came up to me and took my hand in his; placing his hand gently on my bleeding finger he dabbed it with a clean napkin.

"There you go." His face was inches from mine. He seemed to realize and leaned in closer.

I knew where this was going and I couldn't let it happen, "Mark, stop." Just like my feeble attempts a few minutes ago he ignored them completely. Instead of backing up he leaned in even closer. He pulled my face to his with his thumb on my quivering chin. "W-what are you doing, Stop."

Shit, it was too late.

Chapter 20

I sat beside him as he looked at me with an expressionless face. My hand sat on his knee while I looked at him.

"You can tell me, Drake."

He smiled a weak smile, "I know."

Drake:

"Danielle was a girl back home who happened to be pregnant with my child." I said slowly, afraid that if I said it too bluntly Kristen would probably do something illegal.

She sat there frozen to what I had said, Kristen mouthed words but no sounds were heard. I silenced her by pressing a finger to her lips. "Let me finish," I said rapidly, "I was positive that she was pregnant, but my dad insisted she get some tests to prove her point. Let me tell you, that was the best decision of my life."

She looked at me skeptically, "What do you mean?"

"I mean, I didn't get her pregnant, Kristen." A bright smile tugging at the corners of my mouth, she shook her head but a grin was surpassing the frown she had on her cute face. "Whoa. Imagine that. Having to believe you were going to be a father."

I nodded and gave her a light peck on her soft lips, "I told you there was nothing to worry about, Kris. When have I ever failed you?" I asked, giving her a teasing smirk.

She purred and laced her arms around my neck, "Since I've met you..." Kristen held up her petite fingers and began counting. I cupped them and smiled,

"You are a liar." I whispered into her hand, "but a sexy one at that." I winked.

She threw her head back and laughed, "Easy there, Casanova."

"You know you like it, my little kitten." I teased while one of my hands ran up her smooth thigh. "Drake, Mark kissed me."

My hand stopped him dead in his horny tracks.

Kristen:

Drake's hand concluded its journey up my thigh. He nudged my chin and stared at me with his green eyes piercing. "What?"

"Mark kissed me." My voice wandered into a silent whisper.

Before I knew it, Drake was no longer next to me. Leaving a warm aura behind; I looked up in panic and saw him looking around in the house. He was going from left to right until he found what he was looking for: Mark. I ran as fast as my feet could carry me into the house, Drake wasn't standing in the living room nor was he in the kitchen. The bedroom door shut so loudly it left an echo around me, vibrating every wall in its path.

"Drake," I screamed as I jumped over the small futon. My feet were throbbing from the landing; I bolted to the door, hoping for dear life Drake hadn't locked it.

"What the fuck, Mark!" Drake roared from inside our bedroom.

Look what you did now, Kristen. I screamed to myself internally.

Once I was in the room everything seemed to be play in slow motion. Drake's fist extracted, as fast as it had gone up, it came down with such force he knocked Mark oblivious hitting his face with a loud thud. He stood back as he watched Mark's less-than-conscious body hit the ground.

"Drake!"

He turned around, his eyes filled with utter anger. I ran up to him and placed my hands on his heaving chest. His breathing calming down with every breath he took. "Calm down. Please." Drake nodded, although tight with frustration. He pulled me to his side and said dangerously slow, "Get out."

"Is this how it's going to end?" Mark asked while he stood up, his head high as he tried to stop the blood spewing from his nose. I shook my head and took a shirt from the bed, putting it on his face.

"This was unnecessary, Drake," I said quietly, trying to stop the blood gushing from Mark's nose.

Out of the corner of my eye Drake clenched his jaw, shaking his head in disagreement. "Unnecessary, oh you think this is unnecessary. He kissed you, Kristen. How the fuck do you think I am supposed to act?"

I faced him and said, "Not like this."

He didn't answer me, instead he responded to the bleeding Mark next to me. "Why'd do it?"

Mark left my hand dangling as he walked up to Drake, "why can't I have this one girl, Andy?"

Drake:

He asked, barely audible I doubt Kristen heard. "She isn't a toy that can be borrowed. She's a rare jewel, and I'll protect her until my last breath." I said, equally silent.

"But why Drake, why said Mark? You can get any other girl," He insisted. Trying very hard not to land another one on that damn face I said loudly, "You really want to know why?"

He nodded, Kristen looking shocked in the background, "because I love her."

Her eyes went wide when the words escaped my mouth. Not feeling regret of any kind, I said the words again. "I love her, Mark."

Chapter 21

"You--you really mean that?" I stuttered, moving closer to Drake. He smiled sheepishly and nodded.

"Ever sense that one day, I felt something. When it was obvious you hated me, I wanted to do anything to prove to you that I wasn't that cocky asshole. I failed, but at least you know I'm not an asshole."

I laughed silently and looked up, staring straight into those emerald green eyes that always manage to make me melt inside, "There's a thin line between hate and love, Drake. I thought you knew that."

His hands slipped around my hips and tied themselves against my waist, "I love you, Kris."

"I love you too." I kissed him gently on his lips.

"Guys, I'm still here." Mark croaked behind us.

Drake waved him casually and kept kissing me. Mark coughed uncomfortably at our affections, "Do you have any towels, Kristen?"

"Yeah, I'll go get some." I reluctantly let go of Drake and walked out of the bedroom and into bathroom. The small towels were above a counter on top of the marble sink. There was a stool in the corner, I grabbed it and placed it in front of the sink. Standing up on my toes, I grabbed a few towels and went out hastily.

Once I was back in the room the tension was mounting again, "Drake, what's wrong." One look of his face and you would know that something was bothering him.

I reached out to touch his arm, but he soon shrugged it off, "I got a call saying that I have to leave today for some important business."

"What? But the two months aren't even over." I added, starting to panic at Drake's sudden mood change.

"Guess I'll have to leave early. Wasn't that what you wanted since the beginning?" He walked off.

Looking over at Mark who merely shrugged in response, "Drake," I walked out of the room looking around to find him. He was sitting rigidly on one of the bar stools; head resting on his hands. "Drake, what the hell is wrong with you?"

He looked at me, his eyes unreadable, and "I've been thinking--"

"You've been thinking for like 2 fucking minutes. Drake what's wrong?" I pouted. Maybe he was playing with me. Maybe he was doing this to see my reaction. Nobody says I love you then acts like a total douche afterwards.

"I've been thinking, maybe I'm not the right choice for you." He said, totally dodging my last question.

"What's that suppose to mean?"

Drake sat facing me, both of his elbows on the table. "It means that maybe Mark is the better choice for you."

Anger and rejection contorted inside me. After saying those words a second ago, is this what he thinks. Did he just say that to excuse his actions? Was it something Mark said?

"Are you fucking kidding me? After you say I love you? Is there something wrong in that fucking head of yours? You expect me to believe you actually mean that. You don't, Drake. You know you don't mean that!" Angry tears spilled without any warning onto my face. Instead of coming to wipe them away like he said he would, he didn't. He just sat there.

"I do mean that, Kristen. What I said earlier was--was--it wasn't true." Drake stood up and passed me without saying anything else.

"Why are you walking away from me? You are nothing more than a pathetic piece of shit." I screamed at him while he kept walking. "Falling for you was by far the worst mistake I have ever made!"

That statement made him stop fully. "You actually think that?"

I nodded, tears never stopping, "You're making me think that, Drake. The way you're acting right now." He opened his mouth, ready to say something. It wasn't until he looked at my painful motions that he quickly closed it and stomped away without any explanation for his actions.

"Ugh! You're so thick-headed! Is it because I kissed Mark?" I blurted out without thinking.

He suddenly walked back to where I was standing. Drake stood a foot away with nothing but a bitter frown glued to his face.

Drake:

Kristen stood there, ripping my heart with the broken expression on her face. "I'm sorry alright. I should've told him to stop." Tears fell down her face like a waterfall with no end. The sincerity in her voice made it even more unendurable to continue.

"Either way, you can't undo what has been done." I turned myself around and walked off, closing the front door with a slam.

A sigh slipped my lips as I heard the soft sobs coming from the other side of the door. The lump in my throat was unbearably big at this point; my eyes started to burn. I laughed cynically; you caused her this pain, Drake. Feel it burn. I dug into my hair and yelled. She deserved better than me, she deserved someone like Mark. All I did was stand in the way. I loved her, but I was all sorts of wrong for her.

I don't want to let her go. As much as I want to deny it, it's what has to be done.

I turned around and walked away; my heart was hurting like a bitch. If you truly love her, you must be able to let her go.

So that's exactly what I did.

Mark:

After all the screaming--mostly done by Kristen--I finally decided it was safe enough to walk outside without a shield. After I crossed the corner that separated the living room from the hallway, I saw her. Kristen was on the floor, tears getting away from her hands as they spilled onto the floor. Her back moving up and down as her breathing got heavier from crying.

Shit, I have to fix this.

Chapter 22

I picked her up and gently moved her to the futon. Bowing her head with shame she hugged me tightly. "I h-hate him, Mark, I--I hate him so--so--so much."

I smoothed out her hair and said, "Shhh. You know that's a lie, Kristen." She shook her head and tightened her grip.

"No, I'm not lying. Maybe he's right, maybe you're the better option." Kristen looked up with a smile, but her eyes betrayed her. They weren't smiling. They were swimming in sad tears. Heart-broken tears that weren't going to stop until Andrew came and wiped them away.

"You and I both know that you'll never stop loving Andrew." I nudged her chin up. Once she was looking at me, I let her have it, "And Kristen, if you actually believe that Andrew doesn't love you back then you're the one who's thick-headed here. Trust me; I've known him practically all my life. If he had sex with you and actually talked to you right after, then you're something special."

She sat straight up and stared aimlessly out the front window. "Then why did he act like a douche when he left. A simple 'I have to go, but remember what I said' would have sufficed."

"He wasn't lying when he said he had gotten a call, but I know for a fact that it wasn't some damn business call." I told her truthfully.

"Then who do you think it was?" She asked me, her face lit up with hope.

I sighed and rubbed my chin in thought. When I couldn't think of anyone, I said, "The only person who can answer that would be Andrew."

"I don't his have home number, or cell phone number." She said matter-of-factly.

Letting some keys dangle loosely around my index finger I said, "Who needs phones when you can have a face-to-face conversation, right." I smirked, "I'll call Dominic to come and pick us up, from there I'll call in one of my pilots and we can head back to Andrew's house."

Kristen looked at me with a surprised and thankful expression, "Mark, thank you." She wrapped her arms around my neck and hugged tightly. Finally letting go when I told her she should probably pack. Kristen nodded and walked quickly to the bedroom.

Problem fixed, I thought to myself.

*s

When Kristen finished packing her things, we headed out. I took out my sunscreen and rubbed it to my exposed arms. The sun blazed out from the front window making me flinch. Kristen looked worried at my gesture, "are you alright?" She asked, placing her hand on my shoulder for comfort.

I nodded in reassurance and smiled, "Yeah, summer's not really my time of the year."

She looked out at the breath-taking view and smiled fondly, "Too bad. It is for me."

"Well, that's one thing we don't have in common." I laughed and took out my I-Phone, punching in my pilot's phone number. "Ryan, I need a jet, same place, same time."

"On my way, Markus," he said. After hanging up, I took her bags out to the front porch. She followed and sat on a bench.

"I never thought I'd actually like someone like Andrew." She said quietly, staring at the ground.

I sat next to her and said, "People can surprise you."

Kristen laughed softly and nodded in agreement. Looking at the calm ocean and never leaving its waves she said, "Why did you kiss me, Mark? You knew I was with Andrew, so why did you do it?"

I took in a breath of fresh sea air and contemplated my answer. "Kristen, I did mean it when I said I was sorry. Andrew and I—even though we don't seem like it—are pretty close. We were raised together; we bathed together at one point in our lives. He understood me more than anyone." I looked to her and then continued, "When I was twelve, my dad passed away. Aside from Andrew, my dad was the only one who knew what it was like being a normal kid. He built his own empire. My mother's family came from old money, so they knew no other life than the life they lived. Full with riches and fame, but my dad understood I needed to be raised as a normal boy.

"So when my dad died, my mother forbade any connection with Andrew. She said he was a bad influence. Instead, she home-schooled me, didn't allow me to have friends if they weren't good money. Basically, I didn't have any but Andrew and I kept in touch even though my mom was against our friendship. To answer your question, the only time I kissed a girl was back when I was ten. Andrew's parents threw a big party for his birthday. Andrew being the horny bastard he is, gathered all the girls and boys at the party, grabbed an empty beer bottled and put it in the middle of the circle. I had to kiss a girl for my dare. Barely a peck, but it's still a kiss. What I'm trying to say is that I haven't really even kissed a girl. You were standing so close to me, your lips looked so delicious and something else took over. I'm sorry. "I took in another breath of fresh air and smoothed out hair from my eyes.

"Your dad seemed like a nice guy, I'm sorry Mark." She took my hand in hers and squeezed it comforting, "Andrew's still that horny little boy, but at least he is his own person."

I nodded in agreement and smiled, "He was a real ladies' man even back then."

She laughed, "It's hard to imagine him not being one."

"Yeah--" I got stopped mid-sentence when a loud horn honked out of nowhere. We turned our heads concurrently.

A large, rusty boat came our way casually and stopped at the small dock on the island. Dominic stepped out wearing some dark brown shorts and his usual Polo shirt. He waved at us and cupped his mouth, screaming out, "Come, Mr. Parkour! I'll send someone to take the bags!"

I nodded and stood up, giving Kristen my hand. She took it with a small smile as we both walked to the boat. I grimaced as sand got inside my shoes. It was between my toes, making me wiggle my feet until I was able to get rid of it. Kristen laughed at my little motions and said, "Um, Mark is there something...wrong?"

I shook my head and sat down on the warm sand, taking my Vans off I dug out all of the sand. "Fuck." I mumbled.

"Who wears Vans on a beach?" She laughed, clearly enjoying my little scenario.

"I don't like sand, or the beach for that matter," I told her with a frown. Kristen shook her head and smiled.

"You're just like my best friend Sandra. Even though she lives near a beach, she hates the sand and the salty water. All she does is come to the beach to tan."

I patted the sand from my rear end and looked at her surprisingly, "I think I'm in love with your best friend." We both laughed and headed toward the boat. Kristen was ready to clear up things with Andrew, and I was ready to meet this friend of hers.

*

Once we were on the jet, Kristen automatically crashed on the largest seat she could find and slept. Smiling to myself I grabbed a few blankets and put them over her. She moved around until the covers were securely around her. Whether Andrew admitted it or not, Kristen was right for him.

"We'll be there shortly, Mr. Parkour." Ryan's voice rang around the small area.

I sat on my own seat and stretched out my legs, letting out sigh of tranquility. "Mark." I heard a soft voice come from behind.

Kristen lay there, smiling softly. "Thank you." Her eyes fluttered close getting ready to welcome sleep. I turned around and pinned my hands behind my head. Looking outside the window I said, "You're welcome."

Kristen:

The delicate sounds of the jet's engine surrounded me. The events from the night before flooded me, leaving behind a burning hole of sadness inside my shaken body. My heart ached continuo as soon as I thought about Andrew. His face, his hands, his body, his smile, everything hurt just by sparing a mere thought on. The words he said to me kept repeating inside my head like a song with no end.

I trashed around my seat until I was sure I couldn't take it anymore. "Um, Miss?" The flight attendant came in rapidly and smiled forcefully.

"Yes?"

"Can I have bottled water?"

She shook her hair, the smile on her face still intact. "I'm sorry, we don't have bottled water."

I gawked at her, "What?"

She pointed her head towards the sleeping Mark. "Mr. Parkour doesn't allow it. He says it's too bad for the environment."

"Oh. Well, can I have a glass of water...please?"

She nodded curtly and left, leaving me with my thoughts once again. I sighed and looked out the window. Lakes took over pretty much all the scenery. Nothing but water and small patches of land could be seen.

"Kristen." Mark said hoarsely, stretching out his long arms over his head. "What's wrong?"

I didn't answer him right away; instead I kept looking outside the circular window. "Kristen, are you okay?" He persisted. The huge lump in my throat throbbed as I said,

"I don't want to do this anymore. Just take me back home, Mark"

Chapter 23

"Kristen you can't give up! We're less than twenty minutes away!" I stood up and quickly hovered over her.

She jumped up just as quick, "Mark, you don't understand. I thought it was over, and maybe Drake doesn't want me back." Kristen hunched her shoulders and pouted; tears on the verge of being released.

"We went over this already." I told her, "Drake's a dumbass, we both know that, so why the hell are you panicking?"

She sat up and looked me in the eye. "Have you not seen any chick flicks? If a guy says he doesn't love you back then it's pretty obvious he doesn't love you back."

I threw my hands up in annoyance. God, how Drake put up with this is beyond me. "Hollywood, Kristen! Goodness. Lucinda! Get the tape!"

Kristen' facial features twisted with shock horror. She trembled in her leather chair and shook her head violently. "M-Mark, what the--you cannot be serious."

"Oh yeah, Watch me. Lucinda!" I hollered once again. The blonde came in running, apparently worried for whatever reason I was yelling at the top of my lungs with irritation. "Here you go, Mr. Parkour."

"Thanks, Lucy." I mumbled as I turned my attention to the alarmed-looking Kristen. "Now, are we going to do this the easy way...?" I pulled on the tape, showing off the one long string in front of her face provocatively, "...or the hard way?"

She laughed nervously and nodded, "Fine, fine. You win."

"Thought so, and I'm sorry you think I'm a psycho. You're far too important to Drake and I don't want him to be miserable for the rest of his life because he let you go." I sat down with a loud sigh on the seat opposite of hers. I rubbed my temples and rested my head on the pillow behind me.

She sighed as well and said, "You're right, Mark. Look, I'm going to change. Where's the bathroom?"

"Go towards the end of the jet. It's the first door on the left." I said without opening my eyes.

Kristen mumbled a 'thanks' and stood up to get her bags. She left but came back sooner than I imagined. 'Mark!" She growled and began shoving me from side to side, probably thinking I was actually sleeping.

"What? And you didn't have to shove me that hard. I was awake." My shoulders throbbed with light pain came from my shoulders. "That hurt."

"Sorry, I thought you were. Last time I shoved softly you wouldn't wake up." Before she sat down I examined her attire. She changed into comfortable clothing. Faded jeans and a simple tee with her hair tied up in a messy ponytail. Even with that stubbornness Kristen had, I know knew why Drake loved her so much. She was beyond gorgeous even though she didn't try. Add that to the personality she had, Kristen was irresistible to any man around her.

"You clean up...fine." I lied through my teeth. She cleaned up better than fine.

She laughed at my dazed trance and clapped her hands together. "Thanks, and if you try to kiss me again, well, let's just say your crown jewels would be permanently broken."

I laughed loudly but stopped abruptly when she looked serious. Even though she was smiling weakly, she wasn't fooling around. I coughed out loud and patted my groin through my pants. "Uh, I would appreciate it very much if you didn't do that. I promise not to kiss you again...unless it's the cheek."

She nodded happily and rested her back against the seat. "Mark, if we're less than twenty minutes away...then why in the hell is it grass that I see and not buildings?"

I laughed nervously and said, "Um, because Connecticut has a lot of trees?"

She shook her head in disbelief, "Drake lives in New Canaan, Connecticut, Mark. I'm sure they don't have lots of tress because the damn houses are more than acres wide!"

"Okay, I might have lied. But it was for a good cause. We're only an hour away. Here," I picked up the Bloody Gore DVD set and placed it on her lap. "Watch that for the time being."

Kristen squealed and smiled hugely. "Ok, fine. Where's the TV?"

"Oh so you like the sexy stuff. That has sexual content..." I joked but she glared at me; clearly not pleased at my comment.

"Yeah, but it also has hot vampires, blood, romance and hot vampires!" She hugged the DVD set and looked around for a television.

"My goodness, calm down. The television is over there." I laughed as Kristen literally ran to the television. Damn, since when did Kris Skyland become so hot?

Kristen:

I sat with Mark watching Bloody Gore. Gummy worms in my right hand, a Dr. Pepper on the left. I watched as the characters moved about with their problems, but basically staring at Kris Skyland every chance I got.

"If Kate wasn't lesbian I would let her bite me, that and so much more." Mark murmured seductively next to me.

Slapping his arm lightly I said, "Look who the pervert is now! And here I thought you were a good boy."

He took the gummy worm from my hand and stuffed it in his mouth before I had a say and laughed out loud. "I am, but that doesn't mean I can't have my fantasies."

I snorted into my can of soda and busted out laughing. "Ok fair enough."

He pointed out the window and smiled, "We're here, Mrs. Montreal."

I looked at him in shock. "Mrs. Montreal? I forgot about that." Nonetheless I shrugged the thought off and looked in unison with Mark out the small window. Sure enough, we were here. The luminescent lights shimmered significantly below us.

"You ready?" Mark said carefully.

I inhaled a large amount of wanted oxygen and let it out real slow. "Oh yes." I snarled. Fury boiled inside me suddenly. All that was running around my mind at that precise moment was Drake; Drake and his precious neck in my clasped hands.

By the look on Mark's face I was sure my stance and facial expressions weren't the cutest. In fact, I probably looked like a damn psychopath ready to kill. "Uh...Kristen. Please don't turn into Michael Myers while you're with Drake."

"That doesn't concern you, Mark." I said venomously. He obviously took this as a sign to pat me on the back, because that's what he did. "I'm not a dog." I growled at him before he had the chance to speak.

"I know that...trust me I know." He looked me up and down once again and continued. "All I'm asking of you is to give him a chance to explain himself. You'll regret it if you didn't."

Blowing out a breath of air I sat back down and let the jet land before I did anything else. Mark was right. "Ok fine."

"Good, because we're only a few miles away from his house," He sat down joyfully. His smile oozed satisfaction. Well, he can think what he wanted. But when I met Drake, there was going to be more than just talking.

Chapter 24

We had arrived.

Drake:

"Master Drake."

"What?"

"Someone's here to see you."

"Who is it?"

"Turn around," came a low fierce growl from behind.

I did what the familiar voice told me. As I did my breath caught in my throat. I had forgotten how beautiful she actually was, even though her red lips were set into a straight and angry line, she always managed to leave me breathless. Kristen stood near me at the door with furious fumes radiating around her. The deadly vibes could have been felt from miles away. I rubbed my eyes as if I had seen the Tooth Fairy for the first time checking if what I saw was actually there. As I predicted she was, I just wasn't use to seeing Kristen this mad. You're dead, Drake.

Kristen:

Drake could not have looked more shocked. His green eyes bulged at the sight of me. Watching him rub his eyes was the funniest thing I've ever seen. He looked so childish and vulnerable. I wasn't amused at that moment, though. To be honest, I had no idea why I was acting this way. I didn't know why the hell I was so angry. Sadness and hurt were the feelings I should have overcome me, and it did. But they weren't as strong as the fury that vaporized my thoughts.

Drake looked at me with a worried expression, "Kristen..."

I didn't waste a single thought. I tackled him to the floor and began hitting him, letting go of any pain and hurt inside me. To my surprise I felt instantly better, but I kept hitting him. Tears streamed down my face and fell on his. I hit any bit of flesh I could reach. His hands were on his sides doing nothing. He stood still under my hits and looked sad and pained beyond belief. Drake moaned and grunted here and there but didn't do anything to stop me. My punches soon turned to slaps and then began to fade gradually until I stopped altogether. Light pain began to spread throughout my hands as I finished.

I cried on his heaving chest, "Why?" I asked, sobs shaking me from head to toe.

He didn't answer me. All he did was smooth out my disheveled hair since my hair band had fallen off a while ago. Hugging me by my waist he brought me up with him and moved us carefully to his large bed. His strong arms cradled me into a protective cocoon. Drake kissed me delicately on my forehead and hugged me tighter. Both of us were silent, just soaking up the feelings of being together. My sobs became jagged breaths a few seconds later.

Once the tears were dry I sat up and narrowed my eyes at the man lying next to me. "Why? You and I both know what you said were lies—hell, even Mark knew. So why Drake," My eyes began to water, and tears fell once again.

Drake got up and stroked my cheek affectionately, "because I'm a dumbass who takes everything for granted." He said as he reached out to clean away my tears and then placing light kisses underneath my swollen eyes.

"I'm serious," I swatted his hand away, "and you are a dumbass."

A faint and I mean really faint smile played at his lips. It soon disappeared and was replaced by a sad expression. "Kristen, look at me." His thumb went under my chin and nudged. Meeting my eyes he continued, "I know what I did was wrong. I felt like complete shit the moment those words left my mouth, trust me."

I glared at him, "why should I. Just give me one good reason."

"Because I didn't mean them, it wasn't until after I left and boarded the jet that I understood what I had done. Believe me, I meant it when I said I loved you."

"So you expect me to believe you? How do I know you're not just shit-ting with me?" I challenged him with my arms crossed firmly against my chest.

"I'm not. Kristen, you have to believe me. You know me--"

"I thought I did," I cut him off mid-sentence.

He gave me a large heavy sigh and nodded, "Fair. You have reason to believe what you will, but do you want to know the real reason why I said all those things."

I tried to hide my excitement. I nodded slowly. "Tell me."

He moved closer to me and sighed, "The call was from Danielle." He looked at me as to see what my reaction was going to be, when he looked at my expressionless face he continued. "She told me I wasn't good enough for any girl I liked. For any girl for that mattered. She was pissed at me since the tests came back negative. I told her I'd still help her out, but she just cursed me. She told me I was a loser and a sad excuse for a man; and that's when I realized she was right. You were so kind, funny, and beautiful, I knew Danielle made sense."

I wanted to slap Drake so badly right then, but I restrained myself. "Drake, you're better than any guy I have ever been with. Sure you might be a pain in the ass sometimes but you're also sweet, funny and you have a wonderful personality and besides, you have a bigger heart than you get credit for. You are my loser." I cupped his face into my hands and said real quietly, "and on top of all that, Danielle sounds like a bitter little bitch. You should not have listened to her."

Drake gave me a small grin and kissed me, "I know I shouldn't have. But other girls just wanted me for my looks and bedroom ability; you seemed too good to be true."

I pushed him lightly and gave him a serious look, "You are pretty hot, and you are great in bed, but there's so much more to you, Drake. Did you ever think you were too good for me?"

Drake nodded in disagreement and looked slightly angry, "never crossed my mind, Kris."

I sighed; feeling like someone had lifted a thousand pounds from my chest. I felt better in every way possible. The black hole that was slowly eating away my inside was beginning to fade quickly. I felt a hell of a lot better. "Now that we got that settled, I have to go." I tried to raise myself from the bet but he pulled me back by the wrist.

"Where do you think you're going?" He asked.

I looked at him in surprise. "I need to take a shower."

"Can I come?" He asked, but this time with a mischievous grin. I felt giddy inside knowing that my Drake was almost back to normal.

"Tempting..." I mused tauntingly.

Drake didn't like that one bit. He stood up and hugged me, folding my arms across my chest with his. "Now you have no choice but to accept." He whispered sensually against my ear.

"Gee, I'm so glad you're back to normal, honey-bun." I joked with a grin.

He laughed loudly and pecked my neck. "Not quite yet. I've missed you too much for one day. My bed felt so cold without you being next to me. So please, let me join you." Drake batted his eye lashes and gave me an innocent look. I had to conceal the snort that was about to come.

I turned around quickly and knotted my hands around his neck. "Alright then, c'mon, Drew."

Drake's smiled could've cured cancer. It was so big and broad. I took his hand into my own and led him to the huge bathroom across his bedroom. The bathroom consists of a luxurious bathtub in the color of peach, a shower that seemed to be a whole mile long, a comfortable looking toilet and a double sink.

Once we were both inside I turned around and looked at Drake. The smile was gone, but was switched with a confident smirk. His eyes toured my body up and down with admiration. I could tell that by the gleam in his eyes he was ready to ravish me whether I was dressed or undressed. I had to smirk at his lustful gaze. Drake made me feel woman all over.

"Can you wait till I've undressed? You look like a crazy man." I said as I began removing my shirt. My hot pink bra was in full view. Drake grinned and the gleam in his eye became even bigger.

"Any man would be looking at you like this if they got a good look at you, Kris." Drake walked towards me and took off my jeans slowly; savoring the feeling it gave him. He followed the jeans as they slipped down my shaven legs until they were lying beneath me.

Drake licked his lips at my matching booty shorts. "I'm so fucking stupid," He murmured.

I laughed softly and nodded, "Yeah, you are."

He stood up and made a heart motion with his fingers. He smiled and said, "Kristen, you complete me."

I laughed at his little comment. Taking a step back I looked at him up and down. His broad and muscular chest was uncovered, and his jeans hung low on his waist. "Yeah, it's my turn."

I reached out and began pulling his jeans down leisurely. He couldn't get any more excited, and by the looks of it, so did his friend below. Gaining more confidence, I pulled down his navy blue boxers. I smiled at his creeping erection. I wanted to devour him then and there.

"You can't have all the fun," He smirked. Drake then slid his hands around my back and unclipped my bra. Letting the bra fall down to the floor, he pulled down my underwear swiftly. I should've felt all sorts of embarrassed, but I didn't; being naked in front of him in clear light felt normal. It felt right.

After kissing me for a long while Drake took my hand and walked us both to the shower. It was large enough to fit ten people loosely. The stone floor felt cool under my bare feet. As Drake turned the valve to warm he turned to me with the most lustful stare he ever gave me. Water landed on me as it hit the walls and the floor. I guess I looked pretty good to him because the next thing I knew he was pulling me to him. My body melded to his; I was under Drake's hard and large erection.

The passion and desire that filled the shower was so huge it made me dizzy with bliss. His hands roamed freely around my naked body, making the idea of changing my mind impossibility. Drake's touches left behind a fiery trail that couldn't be put out. Every single cell in my body loved Drake to no end at that moment. He was all man.

He squeezed my rear softly as I wrapped my legs around his masculine waist. We both groaned with extreme pleasure as we met. Before he could thrust himself into me he whispered, "You're the best thing that ever happened to me."

Before I could respond he was already inside me, making my answer into blissful moans.

*

We sat on the shower floor with our hands intertwined. The pouring water fell on us both with chilly goodness. It was amazing. Drake was amazing, and he was all mines. I had to keep myself from jumping up and down with happiness.

Drake made circular motions on my flat stomach. We had put on shampoo and other necessities a few minutes ago hastily. Now we were just plain exhausted. To my utter amazement Drake knew how to give great a massage. I sighed in content.

"Master Drake?" said a voice from behind the large door. Drake cursed,

"Yeah," He answered loudly as I kept quiet.

"There were moans coming from the upper level, and your father wanted to know if you were all right?" The butler said, although it was pretty clear he knew what Drake was doing. It had 'sex' written all over it.

I laughed quietly. "Wow, I didn't know we were that loud."

Drake grinned beside me, "I guess we were that good."

I rolled my eyes with a smiled as he answered. "Everything's fine. I just fell and hit my foot, nothing big."

"Alright then, Master Drake," The butler said. His footsteps began to fade as he walked down the stairs.

We both relaxed instantly and breathed out a sigh of relief. "Let's go." I said even though it wasn't what I wanted. The cool floor was so nice I didn't want to get up, but my hands were beginning to look like pale raisins.

Drake nodded in agreement and gave me a hand. He hugged me as soon as I was on my feet. I hugged him back and we walked outside the shower with no hurry at all.

*

I picked up two towels, one to dry my wet hair and another for my dripping body. Drake just needed one, it was a real shame to cover up that handsome body, but he had to, though.

Drake let himself fall on the bed, making it jump up and down. He patted the space next to him and smiled. I did as I he asked, but instead I jumped on top of him. He grunted in surprise and laughed. I straddled his waist and smiled, "I love you." But before I could let him answer I pressed my hands hard against his mouth. "Don't say a word, because I'm afraid if you do you might leave again, you asshole."

Drake laughed softly and before I knew it he was on top of me, smiling like he'd won a 20-mile marathon.

"I love you, too...," He bent down and gave me a light kiss on my nose before landing on my lips, "...and I'm not going anywhere, Kris."

Chapter 25

As Drake and I walked down the stairs at a slow paste, hand in hand, we heard a loud holler coming from the kitchen. As we made it down the many steps we knew where the sound came from: Mark. He smirked over his half-eaten Cheerios. I rolled my eyes and began pouring some Lucky Charms into a sleek white bowl.

"What were you guys doing last night? It sounded like two whales were dying."

I threw him some cereal while Drake smacked his head. Mark's tousled mane went even more disheveled. I opened my mouth to retort but Drake beat me to it. "It's what people do when they're having a great time, Mark. Something you don't know anything about." He snickered, looking smug, knowing Mark, it was probably true.

"So what do you want to do today, Kris?" Drake asked me with a knowing grin.

I looked over at him and smiled back. "I just want to lay in bed and--"

Mark covered his ears and shook his head quickly, "--We don't need to hear the rest, Kristen. I know you two are satisfied with what you see under your--"

Drake and I laughed loudly, "Mark, I was going to say watch a movie. You're an adult, anyways. And my saying the word 'sex' shouldn't do anything like turn you on."

He stuck out his bottom lip and stuffed more cheerios into his mouth. "Shut up." He grumbled when Drake kept laughing.

Drake muffled his laughter with a cough and looked over at me. "If that's what you want to do, then I'm all for it." He grinned once again. Drake and I, in a bed while the lights are down is definitely not a good combination unless you wanted your bed half broken.

"We'll pick out a movie while I wait for Sandra." I nodded and dug into my bowl. Sandra had called me--furious--last night because I was in town and hadn't thought of calling her. She gave me a two-hour lecture on how best friends should be tight and so on. Basically, she invited herself over as soon as she heard the name "Mark". She still hadn't forgotten. I couldn't blame her.

"W-wait, your best friend's coming over?" Mark asked with a hint of shock-horror.

I nodded, "Yup, in about an hour or so."

He looked around, his eyes bulged. "Markus isn't good with the girls, babe." Drake laughed quietly. When Mark didn't protest I knew he wasn't lying.

"Sandra's cool, Mark." I reassured him with a smile but he kept looking around. "There's nothing to worry about except your ears bleeding, she can be pretty loud when she wants to be."

Mark finished his cereal with two huge spoonfuls. As soon as he put his plate in the sink, he disappeared upstairs. I turned look at Drake who was shaking his head with a smirk. "That's Mark for you." I laughed and finished what was left of my Lucky Charms. After I washed my plate, I went upstairs with Drake close behind. I felt a smile creep up. I'd never felt better. His warm body beside mine would forever be welcome.

"So, what do you want to watch?" Drake asked as he settled himself on that very comfortable bed. I would know.

"Hmmm, what do I want...?" I let my eyes trail over his body. Of course he didn't have a shirt on. Much to his advantage, I must add.

"I'm all yours," He said, opening his arms to welcome in a hug. I obliged and hugged him until my arms turned purple. He kissed my hair and turned on the television. I sighed with contentment as he flipped through rows of movies. I finally made him stop on channel 57. I think I might have some competition." He whispered.

"Nah, you have nothing to worry about. Gordon isn't going to come knocking at this door anytime soon." I teased as I turned off the lights.

"You might never know. He could be coming up the driveway as we speak."

I laughed, "Then you might have a problem."

We both just lay there, watching the movie. During the middle, Drake went out to make popcorn saying it was "too much" for him to handle. I rolled my eyes and kept watching. Guns, explosions and guns were probably more his type.

"One bowl of popcorn," He announced as he popped into the room. I shushed him immediately. He rolled his eyes at me and sat back down, wrapping his arms around my waist. I scooted in closer, grabbed a handful of popcorn and crammed it into my mouth.

Drake kissed my cheek and said, "Let's just skip the movie and move on to something more interesting."

I gaped at him. I had no idea why in the hell he was bored. I was practically having the time of my life ogling Gordon. Whatever movie he was watching wasn't the movie I was watching. "C'mon, pay attention to the movie, sweetie." I snapped.

He shrugged off my defensive behavior and closed his arms around me tighter. "I still have condoms left over. Your mom sure knows how to supply."

I felt my face flush with embarrassment. "Yeah, well, that won't happen again. My mom's crazy. As for the condoms, you can throw them away." Damn it, I shouldn't have said that. My whole being was against it.

I muffled his head into the crook of my shoulder, his breath tickling as he exhaled. "I have better plans for them, sweetie. Those plans include you with no clothes, whipped cream and tons of cherries."

I laughed and piled in more popcorn into my mouth, gulping it down with some Dr. Pepper, I said, "I don't want to kill anymore whales, Andy boy."

He took the popcorn bowl away from my hands and put it on the night stand. With a quick motion he managed to tackle me under his wonderful body. Giggles surfaced as I tried to wiggle my way out of his grasped. But there was no way I was getting out, especially when he has that the devilish smirk on his face. He kissed me, and being the expert he is, I lost track of anything running across my mind that very second. All I knew was that his chest and everything about him was only a few touches away. The tips of my fingers were burning for some flesh. Only Drake's flesh I desired.

His hands ran up and down my body like he knew where everything was but didn't get tired of going through it over and over. I had no intention of stopping him, either. "Damn it, Kristen. Why are you so irresistible?" He asked me with broken breaths.

I took in a few breaths myself before answering. "I'm not. It's all in your head, Drake."

He shook his head and kissed desperately down my neck. He pulled up my shirt slowly, resting his head on my stomach. I ran my hand through his hair; his head moved up and down as I breathed. This was how it was suppose to be. Me and Drake, together.

He lifted his smiling head and said, "I have to ask you something."

I nodded, "And that would be?" He stood up and opened up one of the many cabinet doors. He came back with a small, velvet box. Suddenly, my heart quickened. If he was doing what I thought he was doing...He got on one knee. Holy shit, holy shit, holy shit, my body tensed all over. I couldn't talk, I couldn't move.

"Kristen Whitmore..." He opened the box, but my eyes were too clouded to actually see what was inside it. When I finally moved to rub my eyes, I saw it. I immediately burst out laughing. "...will you go on date with me?"

I picked up the pizza coupon and just kept laughing. Tension disappeared. "My God, Drake. What a classy way to ask for a first date."

"I know. I'm a genius." He said, grinning, "So, will you?"

I jumped at him; my arms went automatically around his neck, "Is that really a question?"

"Is that really your answer?" He remarked with a light smirk. To prove my point, I kissed him. And kissed him and kissed him.

"Yes, I'll go out with you..."

"I knew it," He began but I silenced him by touching my index finger to his mouth.

"On one condition," I told him.

"What's the condition?"

"Mark."

He looked at me. "Mark?"

"You didn't let me finish, I meant Mark and Sandra."

His face cleared up, a wicked grin replacing the surprise. "Hmmm, he does like blondes."

I giggled and nodded knowingly, "Yup. It's nice of you to catch up, Andy boy."

He ruffled my hair and jumped onto the bed, sending me straight to his chest; his very welcoming chest. "Please, I was way ahead of you, Kris."

*

We finished watching the movie with minor distractions, and we had to pause it only six times; hardly any. Whew, curse my self-control. We cleaned up our mess, stealing a few glances and smiles of each other in the process. Due to a very complicated situation, Drake and I were going on our first date. When he wouldn't tell me where we were going he'd simply say, "Not going to happen, babe. For all you know it could be the burger joint around the corner." I knew he was lying right there since there wasn't a burger joint around the corner.

Sandra called a little later telling me she was practically stepping in the driveway. But knowing Sandra, she was probably still in Florida. "Still planning on leaving, Mark?" I asked him as he took a banana and began walking up the stairs.

He smiled nervously, like I busted his plans "No, no, of course not. I was just...doing laundry. You know how things pile up."

I shook my head, "Laundry, Alright, then."

With that, he ran up the stairs and hid himself in his cave. Cave meaning his room, because he hardly ever came out of there. I sighed and went back to what I was going, which at the moment was unpacking. Drake came up behind, and grabbed my hands into his. He flipped me around and said, "I would've done that. You panties are well worth it."

I laughed and turned back around to my unpacking when Mark came inside the room looking very pale. "Your friend's here." As he finished he didn't waste a second, he shot out of the room like it was on fire. I looked at Drake who simply shrugged a he's-weird-like-that shrug. I sighed and dropped the clothing back into the suitcase.

I went down the stairs quickly since Sandra was very impatient at times. I got down and opened the door slowly. I had to narrow my eyes as sunlight filled the room, and outside stood my best friend; she was still blonde, still blue-eyed and still Sandra.

Her smile lit me up as she dashed through the door and leaped at me with dashing speed. We tumbled over a bit, but then we just laughed it off like normal. "Kristen! Oh God, I missed you, you little hoe!"

I giggled, "And back at you."

Her hat hit my face as she looked around the room. She was wearing a simple maxi dress with her favorite sandals. "I'm ready for the wedding, and..."

My eyes bulged as her smile turned all devil. "No, Sandra. No, no, no!"

She giggled uncontrollably and nodded, "Oh yes, honey," She threw her hands in the air and gave me a dazzling smile, "and your bachelorette party!"

Chapter 26

"No, Absolutely not." I told her. Sandra just sat on the leather couch, legs crossed, looking bored. Like what I said didn't matter because I always end up losing anyways. I crossed my arms across my chest and sat down parallel to her with a huff.

"And why not, I mean, these are expensive strippers. It's not like they have crabs or herpes, Kristen." Sandra said while looking over her perfectly manicured nails.

"Just because they're expensive doesn't mean they're clean and disease free, Sandra." I retorted.

She sighed, clearly exasperated. "You're coming whether you want to or not. Plus, you owe me about a month of bonding. Do this one for me. Please, oh pretty please, Kristen."

Damn it, she was persistent. I went through all the pros and cons of the situation, but in the end, it was Sandra's pleading face that won me over. "Ok, fine!! But remember I won't enjoy a minute of it."

She clapped her hands together and smiled wickedly, "Oh sure. You say that now."

We both stood up since I promised her a full tour of the house. I took her to the garden, which held more than a hundred types of flowers. We walked into the fountain area with the garden sending colorful shades into the water. God only knows why Drake's always inside instead of being out here. It felt like my own piece of heaven with the light breeze sending cool shivers down my back. I sighed in contentment.

"So, Kristen my sweet, what happened to Mike or whatever?" Sandra whispered to me.

I opened my eyes and looked at her, smiling, "His name is Mark not Mike, Sandra, and uh, he's around here somewhere. He is probably hiding upstairs in his bedroom."

Her face seemed to sparkle at the news, "Then why the hell are we down here?! We should be up there."

I laughed. "My God, just enjoy the scenery will you."

She turned her head from left to right quickly, just like a stubborn little kid. "That's what the Discovery Channel's for. C'mon, Kris. I haven't met a decent guy yet. And trust me, I've been looking."

I sighed and splashed some water at her. She flinched and splashed some at me. We both laughed just how we did every time we did something stupid. "Okay, then. Let's go up." I told her, remembering something. "Oh, and he's very shy. But he's funny and very sweet."

She jumped up and began walking, giving me a thumps up. "Thanks for the heads up."

I caught up to her, draping my arm around her shoulder, "Just be careful with him. He's a knock out, but he has an even better personality."

She snaked her arm around my waist and grinned, "A wonderful personality is all I need."

Amen.

*

Just like I promised, Sandra and I sneaked up the stairs. Whispering and murmuring like teenage girls (technically, we still are teenagers, the whole nine-teen of the word, but it's the thought that counts!). Once we were in front of Mark's infamous door, I knocked but told Sandra to step aside so Mark wouldn't see her. Of course she did what she was told when it was convenient. "Mark, I need help with the dishes. Would you mind helping me out?" I asked sweetly.

"Uh, well, I-I guess." He stammered.

Sandra grinned from ear to ear, a very good sign on her part. "Just let me get dressed."

As soon as he said this, Sandra shook her head. "No! Tell him its okay!" She whispered urgently. I had the urge to laugh, but my cover would've been blown.

"No, it's, uh, it's fine! They're a few dishes, anyways."

"Um, okay." He said sounding confused. Not a moment later the door handle turned and the door opened. Mark wasn't entirely naked, but he wasn't fully-clothed either. He was wearing some basketball shorts that hung low on his waist, and... That's pretty much it. Lucky for Sandra, she loved playing basketball. I heard her give a tiny gasp as he walked up to me, still oblivious about the blond behind him.

"Let's go, then."

Wait," I stopped him, "There's someone I want you to meet."

Sandra popped out of the dark corner and smiled. I mean, really smiled. "Hey there," She said casually and slightly out of breath.

Mark's whole body tensed up. He gazed at her with shock. If that was a good sign or a bad one, I didn't know. Finally he said, "Hello."

If it was some other guy talking, I would've smacked him right then and there. By the look on Sandra's face, so would she." I heard a lot about you, Mark. My name's Sandra." She looked down, suddenly shy. Goodness, she was going for it.

I looked at them both. Mark smiled, "Oh, really? I guess Drake and Kristen love us a little too much because I heard a lot about you, too."

I couldn't take it anymore. I swear I didn't want to do it because it was going somewhat smoothly, but I laughed and laughed to the point where I was nearly rolling on the floor. Both of them glared at me. "What's so funny?" They both said simultaneously.

I wiped a laughter tear from beneath my eye. "Oh, nothing, I going to take a shower, okay. I'll see you both tomorrow."

I wasn't the only one grinning as I walked up to Drake's room.

*

"So did you do it?" My "fiancé" asked me.

I nodded, "Yup."

Drake walked around the bed and sat down in front of me. He beckoned me to sit on his lap, and I did so immediately and without a second to spare. My fingers laced together at his neck for balance. "Do you think we should make it a double date?"

Drake shook his head, "Nah, I want this to be just you and me. I've seen enough of Mark for the past few weeks," He finished with a laugh.

I agreed to this and went out the door the bathroom. Halfway there I heard laughter coming from downstairs. I would recognize that laugh from a mile away. I moved towards the balcony that looked over the living room. Mark and Sandra sat beside each other very closely. Both of their faces beamed. I smiled and walked back towards the bathroom. What a wonderful day this would turn out to be. But then I remembered my so called "Bachelorette Party" and those thoughts soon crumbled into smithereens.

*

"Sandra! I'm supposed to look nice, not look like a slut!" I glared at her from the mirror. She chose my outfit. I had nothing to do with it! The short Daisy Dukes couldn't possibly get any shorter. The bright, neon orange shirt that read "Touch me, I'm single!" could fit a small toddler, and the sandals were hideous and painful. All in all, the outfit screamed "10 bucks and hour!" oh my goodness, this was me being a nice friend.

"Kristen, get with the times!" Sandra said as she smashed some glitter into my cleavage. "You look smoking' hot. This could be the last time you get to dress like this before you get wrinkles and liver spots! As your best friend, I will never let that happen."

Sandra being a blond looked more like Keisha than anything else. But Sandra rocked the look even better. She radiated confidence and wild beauty..."Whatever," I mumbled. "So who did you invite?"

She came behind me and started adding volume into my limp brown hair. "Oh you know...everyone!"

I looked at her with horror, "You what! It was only supposed to be the square, Sandra." Square meaning a group of close friends we had back in high school. Those were fine, but with Sandra's meaning of "everyone" she meant everyone.

"Calm the fuck down, Kris. I meant the square and an extra five or so girls. Not much." Sandra shrugged while adding some hairspray. I coughed at the smell and turned to look at her.

"I don't want anyone finding out about this, Sandra. I wasn't planning on getting married at nineteen, so please be quiet about this." I pleaded.

She nodded in understanding, "Okay, whatever you say." My warm feeling soon changed as her face changed. "Now let's party, hoe!"

Goodness, please, please help me.

We went out of the guest bedroom and began walking outside. Five seconds later we heard a wolf whistle from behind. Not Drake, please not Drake!

"Oh damn it, Kristen. If it wasn't for Sandra holding you like that, I'd lick that glitter right off." I knew that voice all too well.

"Drake, please shut up." I mumbled but he laughed. Sandra - somehow - convinced Mark into getting a bachelor party set up for Drake. Now there he stood; with a normal t-shirt and some plain old jeans while I was nearly naked. Thanks a lot, Sandra.

"Come here." He said, smiling broadly. He tied his arms around my waist, "You look sooo hot, babe. I would unwrap you myself if you didn't have to go. But by the look on Sandy's face, you'd better leave." Drake started calling Sandra "Sandy", when he noticed how much she hated it, he would not stop.

I laughed freely and smacked his chest. "You won't have to do that much undressing. I'm practically naked, and yes, she's like that."

"Drake, we're sorry. I know you want her all to yourself, and I know you're a horny man, but seriously! We have to go!" Sandra said impatiently.

Drake grinned, "I'm not horny."

Sandra simply rolled her eyes and yanked me by the wrist. "Your boyfriend's hot and all, but he could never be like Mark." She whispered so only I could hear.

This time, I was the one rolling my eyes. "Says you." I laughed as she stuck her tongue at me. She-Was-Such-a-Child.

"Take care of her, Sandy!" Drake's distant voice called out.

Sandra huffed and turned around, "My name isn't Sandy! And yes! I'll make sure she's taken care of, you dick!"

We took Drake's laughter as a good-bye. Once we were in the car, Sandra stepped on the petal like her life depended on it. "I hate you, Sandra."

She took this as a compliment and rolled down her window, laughing she said, "I love you, too."

Chapter 27

We arrived at a club in less than 20 minutes. The pink fluorescent lights read: Dare. Let's just say the name didn't soothe the nerves that crashed over my body like a tidal wave. Sandra was Sandra, you didn't know what to expect, and that, of all things, worried me the most. But since this is my best friend we're talking about, I knew she wouldn't make me do anything cringe-worthy. Or at least I hope.

"Woo hood! Now this is what I'm talking about!" Sandra screamed over the pounding music that made the outside walls vibrate to the beat. I sighed and rolled my eyes.

She saw me doing this and gave me a smirk, "Oh, Kristen! Lighten up. Like, seriously! I know you're not usually like this, so c'mon!"

I laughed humorlessly while Sandra paid for our way in. My phone buzzed in my bra (no pockets). I picked it up and answered, "Hello?"

"Kristen, my darling--" It was Dianne, one of the "square", "--Where are you guys?! We're already inside. OMG! You will not believe the guys!" I had the sudden urge to roll my eyes, but I decided I had done that enough for one night.

"We're on our way in. Sandra won't stop jumping up and down with giddiness." I told her and hung up when Dianne laughed.

A thick man with a bushy mustache opened the door with a grim smile. I smiled lightly in return and entered. Holy shit, the music was so loud; it made my insides pound with the rhythm of the beat. I didn't feel like dancing for two reasons, 1. The song was annoying and 2. These sandals hated me.

Sandra started dancing as soon as she stepped her foot in the place. She started to pound; twist and other stuff only flexible people knew how to do. Sandra was a great dancer. It wasn't a total surprise when two guys, both big in the muscle department, started to dance along with her. Their eyes glowed with hunger and lust. Nothing I'd never seen before. Sandra always got that response from men.

This time she just shook her head at both men and came skipping towards me. "Kris! You look hot, and by the looks on the guys' faces, they think so too!"

I snorted and began moving with the beat, "Oh please! I look like a hobo on crack because of you!"

I looked around, and sure enough, some guys where looking at me. Maybe even more than two, I didn't care; it's not like I'd talk to them. I gave them a nod and smiled secretly when they broke into massive grins. "Where's Dianne?" Sandra pointed at a reserved table on the far side of the club. Dianne, Stephanie, Melissa, and Connie were all seated there with a couple of guys and more than a couple of drinks. Connie, the only redhead in our group, clapped her hands when she saw me. All the other girls noticed and all of them came running to me.

Connie was wearing a navy cocktail dress; Stephanie's black hair was pulled back into a pony tail with a plaid mini and a white tank top. Stephanie loved the school girl look. Melissa had torn jeans and a t-shirt (she was the sporty one of the group, but also the wildest aside from Sandra) and finally, Dianne. The infamous Dianne was wearing a tight dress probably shorter than my Daisy Dukes.

Within seconds I was surrounded by the smell of perfume. My eyes were burning severely. "Kristen!" Everyone screamed. There goes my eardrum. I will be totally deaf by the end of the night.

"H—e--y, people," I said real slowly. I rubbed my ears and my poor nose.

They took me by my elbows and dragged me to the table. The guys were huge. I was scared just looking at them. "So, um, what a party, eh."

All of the girls looked at me and broke into tipsy giggles. I picked up a mojito and huffed. "She's not into this, is she?" Melissa asked Sandra in hushed tone.

"I can hear you, Lissa." I told them. They just smiled and stood up, making me follow them to the dance floor. Connie, Melissa and Dianne were grinding around me. Men around the floor stood and stared. I had to admit, this was actually kind of fun. The looks on the guys' faces were priceless. I grinded back. "That's the spirit!" The girls said all together. I giggled and let myself go for once. I picked up a rum and coke and began dancing along with everyone around me. My head was spinning along with my hips. When I stopped, my head was filled with sweat beads and my head was reeling.

"So where are the strippers?" I found myself asking. I picked up a tequila shot and gulped it down as fast as it could slip down my throat.

Sandra took a sip out of her martini and smiled. "Ha! I knew you wanted them, girl"--"No I don't!"--"Sure, but this club isn't the party. It's the syrup underneath the actual sundae." That explained it all.

"So whose house are we going to?"

"Dianne's. You know she has that kickass penthouse at her dad's hotel?"

I nodded, "Well, the men are waiting there!"

"Of course they are." I grumbled, taking yet another shot that Melissa poured. She laughed at my quickness. I was in no mood for fooling around.

After massive amounts of dancing with random guys and grinding with complete strangers, the girls and I thought it was time to go to the real party. It wasn't all that late either, around 10p.m. I lowered the Daisy Dukes and tried to stretch out the shrunken shirt as I rose. Sandra snapped at my hand and dragged me by my arms. I was a bit buzzed but I was conscious enough to know I wasn't drunk just yet.

Sandra, Connie and I went in one car while Melissa, Dianne and Stephanie went in another. Within minutes the car smelled of alcohol and cigarettes. Connie was a smoker. I seriously wanted to throw up. The second-hand smoke didn't do anything to soothe my hurling stomach. "Ugh." I moaned. Resting my head on the cold window I dialed Drake's number. Sandra snagged the phone away from my hands on the second ring.

"None of that, Kris." She smirked, clearly tipsy.

I rolled my eyes for about the millionth time tonight and slumped into the leather seat with a drunken huff. "Whatever." I would be lying if I said I wasn't having fun. I was kind of excited. I always wanted to be in a bachelorette party, I just didn't want to be the subject.

**

Dianne's Dad, Eric Tanner, was a tall man with no expression on his face. None whatsoever. He just walked around as king of the expensive suites and a frown. Of course that frown changed when he saw his wife, Mrs. Gloria Tanner and Dianne herself. "Daddy! This is my friend, Kristen."

He raised an eyebrow, "You're the young girl getting married at nineteen?" Thanks a lot, Dianne.

I blushed deep crimson and nodded, "Yes, sir. Why wait right." Lies!

He nodded like he understood me and smiled a tiny, tiny smile. "Well, enjoy life being single while you can." He waved at the rest of the girls and hugged Dianne goodbye. He left with a cup of brandy in his right hand.

I turned to Dianne and frowned, "Thanks a lot, Anne. Now you're jovial dad knows." I said sarcastically. We all knew her dad was no Santa.

"Oh shut up. At least my dad didn't run off with some stripper." She said, angry.

She wasn't the only one. The alcohol was going to our heads. Something inside me burned. I hated how Dianne was right. I pushed past Sandra and Stephanie, who stood confused, and slapped Dianne right on the face. The smack echoed through the golden lobby. Her hair was all over her face as she touched her cheek. "Shut the fuck up, Dianne. For once in your life think before you fucking speak." I told her, my voice shaking with anger.

A tear slid down her rosy cheek. Connie and Stephanie stood behind her and patted her wild hair. "I'm sorry, Kris."

Sandra was next to me, she rubbed my shoulder. "It okay, Kristen." I didn't know I was crying until she cleaned of a tear from my eye. Another reason why I hate getting drunk. Dianne shrugged Connie and Stephanie off and hugged me. "I didn't mean that, Kris. I totally deserve that."

I sighed and hugged her back. "No, I'm sorry. I overreacted."

She looked at me with a hopeful smile. "Party?"

I smiled, still a bit shaken. "Party."

Much too awkward.

*

Click, went the door as the butler slid the card. Everyone around me, started laughing and screaming in delight as we entered the massive penthouse.

The biggest surprise! Six men were lined together in a straight line. All wearing the same thing: Tight blue Speedos. They had dozens of muscles. Each of them had the same type of tanned skin and they were all brunettes. They smiled once they saw us. True smiles though, they knew they were going to get any action from these hot-ass girls.

"We know you like them with brown hair, Kris!" Wonderful surprise, Comrades!

"Okay, okay. I'll start this. Umm...you," Steph pointed to one of the male strippers. Like the rest,

He was about 6'3 and full of tanned muscle. He had a hooked nose and pretty eyes. "Where do you want me to start, hot stuff." Cheesy and such a turn-off.

I stood up and whispered in Steph's ear. "Not that one! Pick someone else!"

She giggled and nodded, "You're not what I want, now stand back. Hmm, you!" A pretty cute guy stepped forward. He had light hair and a sly smile. His eyes were a type of blue green that you don't get anywhere else. He looked unusually familiar. Below his elbow he had a birthmark. A diamond shaped figure. I gasped.

"Lucas?"

"Kristen?"

Chapter 28

"Oh, you guys know each other?" Stephanie asked with a knowing smile.

"Actually, we d--" Lucas began, but he didn't finish the sentence. "Actually we don't." I finished for him.

"Look, he's going to give me a lap dance in another room, okay." I said.

The room went deadly quiet. "I am?" Lucas said.

"Yes, you are male stripper."

He blushed in embarrassment. "Of course I am."

Sandra came up to me. "Uh, Kristen, I don't think that's a good idea."

"It's just a lap dance. You guys said I needed to chill." I told them. Lucas just stood behind and watched. Before any of the girls could stop me, I snatched Lucas by the elbow and dragged him to one of the many rooms in Dianne's penthouse. I locked the door and glared at him.

"What the hell are you doing, Luke?!" I hissed at him. Lucas was my 1-year-boyfriend back in high school. I ended up losing my virginity to him in the guys' locker room. Yeah, very classy. We were surrounded by the heavenly aroma of sweaty balls. It was the year when I transferred from my old school. Sandra and the girls didn't know how the sweet little virgin loss had it just yet.

Lucas blushed for the millionth time, "I was about to lose my scholarship, Kristen. My mom turned out to be an alcoholic and you know my dad's dead. I needed extra money!"

I smacked his head, "And being a damn stripper was an option?!"

He shook his head and sat on the bed. "It's only for the summer and since Connecticut's far from Florida, I thought no one from my college would be here."

I sighed and hugged him. "Luke, I mean, you know you look hot, but seriously, a stripper? A janitor would've been more...well, more."

"I saw an opportunity and, Kris. It's actually good money." He said with a small smile.

I laughed and hit his bare thigh with my knee. "After this, I want you to go home and find another job."

He nodded, "Yeah, I figured. But..." He trailed a tall finger up my thigh, "You are Kristen Whitmore."

I picked up his finger and kissed it before I placed it on the bed. "Yeah, and I'm also in a relationship so back off, honey."

He sunk his elbows on the bed; his whole body leaned towards me. "Who's the luck guy?"

I stood up. "Drake Montreal."

He snorted. "Of course." He walked up to me and gave me a small kiss on my cheek. "Have a good life, Kris, you deserve it." Lucas turned around and walked out of the door. Even though the music was on, you could still hear the front door closing.

*

I pulled the shorts down and sighed. I went out and looked around me. The term 'guys everywhere' was an understatement. It wasn't an orgy, but it sure wasn't a family dinner. Sandra ran to me and eyed me curiously, "What was that all about?"

I didn't want to explain so I shrugged, "I'll tell you later, okay?" She nodded and turned back to the party.

I sighed and went to sit by Stephanie. She slapped my knee and pointed towards the door. I smiled sheepishly and turned to look at the show. Dianne was chasing a guy that managed to take away her shirt. She jumped up and down with tipsy happiness. I groaned and sank deep into the seat. My party mood was ruined.

"We can leave if you want," said Sandra.

"No, no, I'll wait till it's over."

She smiled and started to skip with glee. "Okay, everyone! Dim the lights, turn on the fog machine, and bring out 2 guys!"

I gasped as Sandra's evil smile spread from one ear to the other. They weren't going to make me do this. They were my friends for fucking sake! Only when I saw the gleam of mischief in all of their eyes did I truly know my so called "friends" were not on my side for this one.

"Oh Lex--xis," Melissa sang out. "Come sit with us!"

Just one look at them told me I had to. I grimaced and sat down in a plain wooden chair. "Guys..." I said slowly.

Before I could react, they tied my wrist with lacy g-strings. I screamed out, "Guys! I think this is going way overboard!"

They just giggled. They just fucking giggled! The lights were eventually turned off when they knew I wasn't going anywhere. The music started and the guys appeared in front of me. They were tanned, sweaty and muscular. Too muscular.

"Okay, are you ready for this?" One of them asked with a slight accent. I laughed nervously, "Look, I'll pay you double if you back away--"

"Don't listen to her, we'll triple it!" Sandra yelled happily.

The guy shrugged and smiled at me, "There's your answer."

At once, both guys started to dance. I held my breath as they started moving towards me. They popped their jewels everywhere and for a minute, I thought they were going to go nude. But that was a bluff for the drunken girls in the audience.

They rubbed themselves on the chair, on my legs and on my arms at one point. I. Was. Going. To. Throw. Up. No joke.

They each put a leg on the poor chair and started to really pop...in front of my face! I gagged for air, because frankly, it was stuffy and the guys smelled like sex. "I am going to die!" I screamed dramatically.

It was no use of course. But after about five minutes of this, they finally stopped. Thank God!

I learned that their names were Rodney and Ramon. There was no way of escaping it since the girls made a little song about us. They let go of my hands and patted my shoulders. "You took it like a champ!"

I glared at whoever said it, but after a moment I smiled. "I'm going to take a long shower when I get back to Drake's. Wouldn't want to get caught with unwanted hair and sweat now do we."

They all laughed. Connie grinned, "So, how's life with Drake? Is it like they said it was?"

I frowned, "Who's 'they'"

Her smile faded, as well as the others. "You know, back when he was a player. Girls kept saying he was a sex god and all in the magazines."

I had forgotten Drake had a past with dozens of other random women. He has changed so much since I met him. "Oh. Well, I don't kiss and tell. Sorry Ladies!"

They whined and whined...and whined some more. Sandra already knew this, so she was just relaxing and watching the show play out. "Please, please, please!!" They all yelled in unison.

"Fine, only because I love you guys" --"Yay!!" --"He's..." Pause for dramatic effect..."He's beyond wonderful!"

They broke into loud giggles.

*

The party got cleaned up, all the strippers went out. Melissa, Connie and Stephanie got a cab to take them home. It was only me, Dianne, and Sandra still there. "Well, thanks a lot for letting us use this place, Anne." Sandra told her as she gathered all her things.

Dianne nodded and kissed us both on the cheek. "No worries, take care, babes!"

We hugged good-bye and finally, Sandra and I were out the door and headed home. I sighed dreamily, in a few minutes I would be in Drake's bed lying next to him. I pulled out my phone and dialed his number. Drake picked up on the second ring. "Hey, babe." His voice was sexy and rough from sleep. I looked at the time, 12:32. Great, I woke him up.

"Sorry, I woke you up." I said as I bit my lip.

He chuckled, "its okay, what's wrong?" Its amazing how one voice can make my body radiate with heat, my knees feel like jell-o and he makes my heart beat twice as fast. Just to hear his voice makes me calm and feel loved, only him.

"Nothing. I'm headed back to your house. I guess I didn't want to wake anyone up. Can you open the door so that I won't make much noise?"

Drake laughed softly, "I'll be waiting for you, Kris, and my bed is seriously missing you. I couldn't sleep without you beside me,"

I giggled. Sandra gagged. "Don't worry; I'll be there in no time."

"I'm counting on it," Drake said sensually.

I hung up and sighed. I loved that man. Sandra walked silently by my side as we were looking for the car. Once we got in and got the heater turned on, she gazed at me and asked, "Who is Lucas?"

"The guy I lost my virginity to, I guess I needed to talk him out of that miserable job."

"Oh, in that case, then I'm glad."

The car rumbled to life. Sandra steered out of the hotel's parking lot and headed towards the freeway. Nobody talked, which was out of character for Sandra and I. "Okay, Sandra, what's wrong?"

I turned to look at her and was surprised to find her eyes welling with tears. "Are you crying?"

"Yes," she said, her voice wobbled with tears, "Kristen, how about if you trade me for Drake. I mean, I love the fact that you're happy but how about if I don't see you again?" She wailed dramatically.

"Sandra, it's not like that! You're basically my sister!" I tried to console her.

"Really? Then why didn't you tell me you lost your virginity to that totally hot guy. You transferred for a year, Kristen, you came back and you didn't think of telling me. I was proud I lost my virginity before you did. Ugh, it was all a fluke!"

I groaned, "Sandra that was like three years ago! And I'm sorry, I just felt like crap afterwards. I'm sorry."

Sandra sighed and cleared a tear. "Fine, but you and I are not on speaking terms until tomorrow."

I rolled my eyes, "Whatever."

I looked out the window. The cars' lights turned into paths of luminescent brightness. Surprisingly, the sounds of cars zooming made me calm. My eyes felt heavy with exhaustion. My head began to blank itself with sleep. I was about to go under when a strong glow made my eye lids pop open. It was all I could see; the night sky seemed to be eaten by this light right in front of me.

Sandra screamed. Her eyes were so horrified my spine shivered.

I didn't hear the impact because I was too busy marveling at the things around me. Glass shattering into a million pieces, metal bending like it was doing gymnastics. The ragged lighting twisted and reflected off the tiny portions of glass, making them resemble the tiny dots of light on the sky.

It was Sandra's shocked and ear-splitting screams that broke my thought. This scenery had nothing beautiful about it, far from it.

I was surrounded by a cluster of debris. But that changed; everything around me was nothing more than darkness. A darkness that surrounded every wall of my vision.

Drake...

Chapter 29

"Sandy calling, Sandy calling! (Phone ringing)"

The loud and obnoxious ringtone blazed my room with unwanted sound. My ears peaked with annoyance. "What the hell," I hissed.

"Sandy calling, Sandy calling! (Phone ringing)"

The ring just kept on going. My hand was as blind as my eyes were. The dark room gave no clue as to where the damn phone was. Then I remembered I left it next to me on the bed in case Kristen was to call. I sighed in content. To think she was going to be next to me in a few seconds made my irritated attitude become calm. I cleared my thoughts and put on the sexiest accent I could make up, "Hello, beautiful."

The voice on the other line didn't talk. There was whimpering and panting, like the person had been crying for the past decade. "Hello?" I said again, dropping the fake accent.

The voice sniffed and when it spoke, it was thick and heavy with tears. "A. A. A. And-drew?"

It was Sandra like I never heard her before. His high and usual cheerful tone was replaced by grief and anguish. "What's the matter?" I found myself asking.

The hottest pit in hell couldn't warm the cold feeling that swept over me, it nearly knocked me over. "I-it-it-it's Kr-K-Kristen, An-Drake. Sh. Sh. She, she..." Sandra wailed out.

My hair was dead, limp and lifeless on the floor below me. "What happened, Sandra? What the hell happened?" I shot out of bed and ran out the door.

"S-s-she was hit, Drake. She's in a c-c --"

"Spit it out, Sandra!" I yelled.

"She's in a coma!"

I wasn't in my home anymore. Everything that surrounded me blurred and escaped my vision. The phone hit the floor with a thud. The blood drained out of my body and the devil himself was holding it above my body with a smirk. I didn't know I was running until I was face-to-face with Mark's door. My fist was pounding on the hard wood until I could smell blood rising off of my knuckles.

"You, man, what the fu--"

"Give me the damn keys to the fucking car!" My roars echoed around the hallway. I was panting like a bull and for the first time since my mom death, tears trickled down my face.

I didn't give a damn if Drake Montreal wasn't supposed to cry. Kristen was the exception to everything. The hot tears poured out of my eyes in disruption. Kristen's face flashed in my vision, her beautiful smile replaced by the deep frown of a coma. I shuddered. My stomach felt hollow and there was an unmovable boulder stuck in my throat.

Mark opened the door, his brows scrunched in confusion. "What happened, Drew? Why so worked up?"

He threw me the keys and without a second to spare, I bolted down the stairs. "Kristen...she's in the hospital." I said meekly, but I knew he heard me. His stomps behind me told me he was following.

My dad appeared at the bottom of the stairs, rubbing his eyes in surprise. "What's going on?" I growled and pushed him aside. Kristen needed me and I was just wasting time.

I opened the door to my Lamborghini Concept S. I started the car and kicked the petal like my life depended in it. This in a way was true. Because without Kristen, my life would be useless and there would not be a reason for living anymore.

Sandra

"Drake calling! (Phone ringing)"

I picked it up on the first ring, "He-hello," I said, my voice grew hoarse. Just looking at Kristen made me break out crying.

"Sandra! What hospital is she in?" Drake bellowed from the other line.

I dabbed my eyes with tissue and spoke, "Nordic Regional," I made it come out crystal clear.

The line is dead.

I sighed and looked over at Kristen. My eyes overloaded with tears. I sobbed into my hands, knowing this was my fault.

Drake

I stepped on the petal and made it go forward as fast as I could, the hell with the Police.

I got to the hospital in record time. The car door opened smoothly and when it fully opened, I ran the fastest I could. People all around me looked at me like I was insane. It might have been true.

A woman in her late thirties asked if she could help me. "Kristen Whitmore." I was choked up.

She looked into her computer and ordered me to follow her. I did so, but her slow pace was killing me. Couldn't she move any faster? She came to a halt in a room with the door opened. She left me with my thoughts clouding my mind.

What is she's gone? What if I hadn't come in time? What if I didn't like what I saw? What if she was awake? I shrugged off all those thoughts and walked into the room. Sandra was by her side, still crying into her palms. Her fragile body shook in unison with her sobs.

"Sandra."

She looked up, both of her eyes were red and swollen, but the left eye was black. Like a boxer landed one on her. Sandra's nose was going pink with the tissue rubs and her hair was a complete mess, her lip quivered uncontrollably, and she was tainted with dried blood all over her arms. She stood up and limped towards me. My whole body was numb. "Oh Drake," She cried into my chest. "I'm-I'm so sorry."

I patted her head and hushed her. I made her sit back into her chair.

I turned around and stopped. Kristen was just there, lifeless as a puppet without strings. Her arms were bruised with purple spots. Her beautiful face was covered with tiny scratches, her forehead covered in dry blood. Her lips were dry and colorless, her tanned skin pasty. Maybe there was more damage I couldn't see.

Before I knew it, my knees were on the floor. The lump in my throat became tears and the hollow feeling became present again. I grabbed her bruised hand and kissed it. She looked beautiful even though she was a wreck.

I kissed her stale lips and her bloody forehead.

A doctor came in. His mouth was set into a straight line. "What's the verdict?" I whispered.

"Broken ribs, minor cuts and bruises, fractured elbow and head trauma. She'll be fine if she wakes, Mr. Montreal."

"What do you mean if?" I asked him darkly.

"We are unsure how long she will stay like this, Mr. Montreal." The doctor said seriously, "She suffered minor head trauma, we hope it won't be long but we could be wrong."

I glared at him with all the hatred I could muster. "You're not sure? You're the fucking doctor. You should know."

Sandra came up behind me, "Drake, stop."

The doctor looked at me with knowing eyes. "I know you're worried, Mr. Montreal, I understand how you feel. But acting this way does not solve anything."

I sighed knowing he was right. He soon left but a few other people came in to check on her. They drew blood, and she didn't jump. They changed her pillow, but she kept the same blank expression.

"Drake,"

I looked up to see my dad and Mark, followed by Kristen's mother. She was crying.

"Everything is going to be fine, son." My dad said while rubbing my shoulder.

I nodded. I had to be strong for both of us.

Chapter 30

"You should go home and rest, bro. We'll stay here." Mark told me over Sandra's head. She was tucked neatly in the crook if his shoulder.

I shook my head and turned my attention to Kristen, "I'm good. You two should go."

"If you think I would leave her side Drake, then you're wrong." Sandra's fragile and broken voice said. She raised herself up and looked me in the eye. "You're not the only one here that's worried for her, you know. I care for her as much as you do."

I snorted internally, "I doubt that."

Tears welled up in her eyes again, "You should stop acting like such an ass and just go home and get some rest. As much as I hate you right now for saying that, she wouldn't want you to die of fatigue."

I glared at her, "You're worked up. I'm not going to argue with you, Sandy."

Mark enveloped her in his arms and soothed her. I looked at the scene longingly. What if Kristen and I never get to feel each other's caress again? "It won't kill you to have faith, Drew."

"Who says I don't have faith?" I snapped.

"You're actions, said Mark" he stood up with Sandra in his arms and carried her to the vacant bed on the far side of the dark room.

I sighed loudly and placed myself next to Kristen. Her expression never changed in the last fourteen hours I was here. She was still blank, like someone erased all her emotions. My heart ached every time my eyes managed to look her straight in the face. Maybe Mark was right. I didn't have enough faith.

"We brought coffee." My dad said softly. He handed Mark one and brought another one for me. Eliza was trailing limply behind him. Her face was lacking color and her eyes were swollen and crippled with depression. She always looked down when she entered the room. Guess she didn't want to see Kristen like this.

The Styrofoam cup was right in front of me, alongside an oatmeal cookie, but I pushed them away. "You have to eat something, Drake."

"I'm not hungry, dad."

"Yes you are." He insisted.

"Would you mind shutting up?"

He flinched at the harsh comment and sighed. Eliza pulled on his sleeve and both of them left with Sandra and Mark. "Asshole," I heard Sandra whisper.

At this point, I really didn't care. They could say or do anything they wanted, but I wasn't leaving her side. I grabbed her hand and kissed it. The skin was smooth and yet so cold. I pulled over a chair and rested my head on her stomach, closing my eyes and falling asleep to the beating of her heart.

*

"Oh, Mr. Montreal, Mr. Montreal."

My eyes fluttered open. I was sleeping on an empty bed. "Where's Kristen?"

The nurse giggled and went behind me. She looked eerily familiar. "Her?" She giggled again and rubbed my back with her long fake nails seductively. "She's dead!"

Her cleavage popped out of her uniform, her hands turned into claws. The whole world came crushing at my shoulders, knocking the breath out of me completely. "No, no, no, no! She's not dead, she can't be!" The pain was too unbearable. She wasn't dead. She just wasn't.

"Oh but she is, baby! She really is! Her body couldn't fit in the coffin, so I ripped her limb from limb; real fun actually." She laughed again...and again and again until I couldn't take it anymore. I pushed her hard against the wall.

"You're lying! Why the fuck are you lying!"

She began stripping off of her uniform, when she looked up; I finally knew who she was. Danielle.

"Drake baby, we can finally be together, you, me, and our child."

I laughed darkly and spat in the opposite direction. "I will never be with you, Danielle. You're nothing more than a manipulative and shallow bitch. I feel sorry for the poor kid. He has to live with you as his mother."

Her flirty smile turned into a scornful sneer. She screamed and charged towards me. "She's dead, Drake. She is dead, dead, dead."

I shook my head vigorously, "You're wrong."

She smirked and licks her lips. "Look at the bed, honey."

I did what she said, and sure enough, Kristen was there, bleeding and lifeless. "NO!"

.....

"Drake, Drake! Wake up!"

My eyes snapped opened. My heart raced, my shirt was drenched with sweat and I was panting like an angry bull.

It was only a dream, only a dream; only a damn dream.

I looked down, Kristen's hand was red. "Look at what you've done!" Sandra screeched.

I finally noticed that I was holding onto her hand so tight, I left it bruised. "She's still here." I kissed her forehead and smiled lightly. She was still here. And as long as she was, I wouldn't let anything else happen to her.

"Of course she is! Look, Drake, I'm sorry I put you on blast. I'm just so worried and I-I --"

I hugged her, "its okay, Sandy. I was an asshole, just like you said."

She pulled away, "Go and get yourself a coffee if you really aren't going anywhere. It'll help."

I nodded and gave Kristen a final kiss before I left the room.

It was only a dream.

I walked around aimlessly until I found the hospital's cafeteria. There was no line and only a few people were scattered around the tables. I picked up some chips and a cup of coffee. After a moment, I knew I was lost. "Excuse me," I asked a nurse a few yards away.

She turned around and smiled, "Yes?"

"I'm looking for room 14-D. I am lost."

She laughed and came up to me. "Follow me, hon."

A few seconds past before she spoke; "Are you by any chance Drake Montreal?"

I nodded, "Yeah, that's me."

In lightning speed her mouth turned into a flirty grin. Great, just what I fucking needed. "You know, I'll be done with my shift soon."

"Good for you." I said with a frown. Apparently she still hadn't gotten my drift.

"You wouldn't mind coming -"

"Actually, I do mind. My girlfriend's in a coma, and I don't want to have sex with you." Shit, was I really this much of a player? "Just point me in the direction of the room."

The nurse was silent, but she led me to the room either way. "I'm real sorry about that." She whispered.

"Don't be."

I walked in and sat next to Kristen. Sandra, Mark, my dad, Eliza and five others I didn't know were crowded around her. Sandra introduced me, "Drake, this is Dianne, Melissa, Stephanie, Connie and Lucas."

Lucas? Why did that name sound familiar.

Chapter 31

Hey, dude." Lucas extended his hand in my direction. I shook it and stared at him in the face.

"Who are you?" I finally asked.

Lucas blushed and nodded. "I, um, used to date Kristen in high school." The room went quiet, waiting for my reaction.

I thought back and dug into my memory. I remember Kristen told me about him...on the island. Of course, the guy she lost her virginity to was Lucas. No wonder the name sounded so familiar. I nodded and turned to look at Kristen. A week ago I would've felt jealous, but now I saw no use to it. For the millionth time a speck of hope rose inside me, hoping Kristen's eyes would magically open. But like the millionth time, I was disappointed.

The room shuffled with sound, but I didn't see any movement. My focus was only on Kristen.

"We're going to the cafeteria, Drake. We'll be back in a few." Mark's voice rang out from the doorway. Like I care, I thought to myself bitterly.

My chin fell again to her belly. I breathed in the hospital smell that has consumed her whole body, but a hint of her intoxicating aroma still managed to remain. I really needed her scent in my life again.

My eyes drifted from her lips, to her eyes. Memories of our time on the island washed over me, a smile tugged at the corners of my lips. How she loved the sweets I told Ricky to order, the swim at night, the arguments we had, the flirty times and our first time. It seemed like a year rather than months.

Then it happened. Her finger moved.

I leaped up and smiled hopefully, everything inside me swelled up with happiness and hope. "Kristen babe, Kris, I called" I wiggled her fingers back and forth but her eyes never opened. I growled and called out to the doctors. They came rushing in.

"She moved! I saw her." I told them meekly. My deep voice broke. Like a little 12 years old.

The doctor shook his head, "That happens, Mr. Montreal. It can be pure coincidence or just a thing of the moment."

I dug my fingers into my head and kicked a wooden chair as hard as I could. "What the fuck! I saw her move!"

All the nurses let their eyes fall to the floor. What a pity. "I'm sorry, they said."

I sighed loudly and soon the team of doctors went out the door. I sat down next to her and grabbed her hand softly, like the softest petal and as cold as ice. I hated the feeling. My head dropped on the bed and I fell asleep with the hopeful feelings crumbling to smithereens.

Days passed like cars rushing by on the street. Kristen hadn't moved nothing seems to have changed. Her family came and went leaving behind their well wishes, some flowers and get-well cards. I was a robot for most of the time. I hardly ate, hardly slept and hardly noticed anyone.

Everyone else seemed to be worried about my well-being. All I could do was shrug them away. Kristen was practically dead and they thought about me.

Before I noticed, it had already been 3 weeks. Three miserable weeks that felt like a century.

"Drake, you do realize you've only been home for like, two days right? Kristen will be fine, man. You should go to your house, sleep in your bed and shave off that creepy beard that's over covering your face." Mark was standing beside me; his hand was on my tense shoulder.

"Go get me a razor then."

"Drake, that's not the point. Get your stubborn ass out of here and get good night's sleep for once. You look like you're on the verge of death. Kristen wouldn't want that."

I stood up and went out the door. "Why the hell do people drag Kristen into everything, huh?"

"Because it's what she would've wanted. You know she wouldn't want you to worry for her as much as you are." He angrily replied.

I looked down at my body. My usual muscles were less noticeable; my face looked gaunt and overall, depressed. Maybe Mark was right. "Whatever."

"Sandra's coming over in a few minutes. She can stay with Kristen while you and I go get something to eat, and get you to a damn barber. You're starting to look like Jesus, bro."

My rusty lips curved into a smile. It felt so strange, but I missed it. "There's the Drake I know." Mark said as he noticed my smile.

"Fuck off," I pushed him in a tease and went back into the room. Sandra came in a few minutes as Mark promised. She looked sad as her eyes settled on Kristen. She was wearing some dark shorts and a loose t-shirt. In the past few weeks, she hadn't bothered to dress up. Jeans, shorts and t-shirts were all she wore these days.

"Go get some sun, Drake." She said with a light smile. Has anyone not noticed my damn appearance?

I nodded frigidly and walked out of the hospital with Mark. Once we were in his new BMW I sighed. "So what's up with you and Sandy?" I asked, trying to make small talk even though I really just wanted to sleep.

Mark's face lit up, as it usually did every time someone talked about Sandra. "It's going fine. She's great."

I rolled my eyes and opened the car window, letting cool air wash over my face like a shower. "I'm happy for you, Parkour."

He nodded and kept on driving. A couple of minutes into the drive, we arrived at the house. I opened the door and made a beeline to my room. I grabbed a pair of jeans and a sweatshirt before going to the bathroom to take a much needed shower. The pro-of-a-barber butler will give me a much needed shave and trim, I met Mark in the kitchen.

"I'm starving."

"When in the hell are you not?"

He laughed, "Go to hell."

We ate and talked about random shit from our childhood to recent events, dodging anything related to Kristen. After we were finished, we headed back to the hospital. I'll admit I felt a hell of a lot better even though the food tasted like paper.

"Did you guys have fun?" Sandy asked while standing up to give each of us a hug.

I nodded truthfully and grumbled, "The best I had since two weeks ago."

I settled back beside Kristen and heaved a sigh of relief. Mark and Sandra parted ways and left me to my thoughts. I leaned back into the chair and stared at nothing in particular. Before I knew it, my head was in my hands. I cursed till my eyes filled again with tears. Since when was I such a fucking pansy?

My mom's face flashed into my mind out of nowhere. Her pale blue eyes, her tanned skin, her kind smile. I missed every single one of those things about her; just as I did Kristen. I mulled over what life would be like without Kris but quickly thought of something else. The thought was too much to bear.

I closed my eyes and cleared my head; letting the salty and useless tears fall where they may.

"Since...when....does...Drake Montreal...cry. Is this my Drake?" A deep hoarse and broken down voice called out to me weakly, making my heart race and thump as loud as a monster truck. I opened my eyes ever so slowly.

My breath caught inside my throat. Time seem to have stopped; everything around me lost balance. And for a moment, I dare say it; I think I would've fainted. Something deep within me exploded into thousands of happy faces dancing around in a relief and extreme bliss. Was I making this up because it was something I so desperately wanted to see?

For a few seconds I just sat there in blissful shock. The gorgeous angel was just looking at me with an amused confusion, her eyes drooping with exhaustion. I gasped. "L-L-Kris!"

She snorted weakly, "Duh, sweet tart."

I wanted to jump up and down. I wanted to run miles and miles, because the sudden energy and ecstasy that surged through me was so unbearable. My face ached with the smile that encircled my face.

Her smile was playful, but behind that was slight pain. She rested her head on the pillow, "Are you going to stand there...or are you going to tell me why in the hell do I feel like complete shit?"

I loved this girl so much it was thoroughly ridiculous.

Chapter 32

"You have to eat, babe." Drake called out to me from the room's hospital.

I pouted to no one in particular and huffed. I was in pain, my head was being pounded over and over by a large hammer, my feet and arms felt like jell and I looked like complete and utter shit. Food was something I didn't have in mind. "I'm not hungry, Drake."

As I found out the day before, I was in a coma for three weeks; three whole damn weeks. Drake's expression when I had opened my eyes made my heart ache every time I thought about it; but from the look on his face, I knew he really cared about me. And that was all I needed. Sandra came last night too. She's not famous for her crying, but when she saw me, it was like hurricane Katrina all over again. She hugged me repeatedly and blamed herself and asked for my forgiveness.

I laughed and hugged her even tighter. I was the one who should feel guilty for making everyone grieve, I told her. Mark was happy to see me awake as well. He told me the story of The Crying Drake. If it wasn't so sad and heartbreaking to see my Drake torn up like that, I would've giggled.

Drake came out of the bathroom in a few seconds. The change was really noticeable actually. He looked skinnier and less healthy, his eyes lacked that cheerful humor, but I could see it coming back. But even with all the change, he was still fine as hell. Any girl within a mile would jump his lovely bones, but as fate has it, he was only for me.

"Yes you are firecracker. Just eat something, alright." He kissed my forehead and got me some yogurt from the food tray a pretty nurse had given me that morning.

"Fine, only for you."

He smiled, "You shouldn't have to eat because of me, but because of your health."

I snorted into the yogurt, which I knew looked nothing close to attractive, especially with the way I looked now, but I just had to. "Then why did my coma keep you from eating, huh?"

Drake laughed and jumped onto the couch beside my bed and sighed happily, "Because that's different, baby. I love you, Kris, and now I know how much, I really do."

I blew him a kiss, "I love you too, and since I'm Kristen, I already know how much I love you."

Just then, Mark and Sandra came into to room holding chocolates, flowers and a banana and strawberry smoothie. "Whew, this is enough of this love-dovey talk! It sickens me....it just sickens me!" He fell to the floor dramatically while Sandra kicked his thigh, Drake threw him a pillow and I threw him some of my yogurt. "Whoa, easy, people. I was only fucking around."

"Well go fuck around somewhere else, Mark." Drake smirked.

Mark flipped him off and kissed Sandra; and not just a simple kiss, oh no. He kissed her hard and passionate; with tongue and lots of touching. This time, it was Drake and I who threw a fit. They laughed and Sandra retorted, "Like you two don't do it. Actually, I'm positive it's even worse."

I blushed and shook my head slowly. "Nope, it's perfectly innocent. Isn't it Drake?"

He laughed and stood up proudly. "Oh come on, Kris. We don't have to lie to our best friends! We do it stronger, more passionate and probably even better. You know, more experienced."

He wiggled his eyebrows at me and I actually went along with it. "You're right, Drake. We don't have to lie to them. I'm sorry for lying, you guys."

Both Sandra and Mark's hand went up in outrage, "You two are impossible!"

To get them even more ticked off, Drake slid his hand behind my neck and drew me in for one of those passionate kisses we were talking about, and boy was it passionate. "Ouch, ouch, ouch" I moaned in pain when the kiss got a little bit too heavy and ended up hurting one of my many injuries.

"Shit, sorry, babe." Drake said nervously, he went around and got me another pillow to stash under my head. I smiled fondly up at him and kissed his soft cheek.

Sandra clapped her hands to get my attention and said, "So, about this whole wedding thing..."

Drake cut in, "We don't have to have a wedding if you don't want one, Kris. You're torn up and - "

"No, I'm fine. The doctor said I was going to be brand new in two weeks time. I just don't want it to be a big one wedding. Just a small one."

He nodded, "Whatever you want, babe."
******

13 days later

I walked around my hospital bed with a grim smile. Hopefully I wouldn't see this wretched bed ever again. The mirror that one of the nurses let me borrow sat at the foot of the bed. I looked at myself and smiled. The black eye was gone, and the bruises on my arms and legs were hardly noticeable. I was grand, and I loved every single moment of it.

"Are you ready to go or are you moving in?" Drake asked with a bag full of my clothes and a smirk. I drank in this vision. Over the past week, Drake was really hitting the gym. He added the muscles he loss and gained a few more. I sighed dreamily. Gosh was he hot.

"Of course not; let's get the hell out of here." I set the mirror down and walked towards him with my arms extended. He let his hands slide behind my waist before lifting me up into a big bear hug. His scent filled my nose with that familiar smell. Mmm. I was never going to get tired of breathing around him.

"Mmm, you smell nice," I told him with a kiss.

He smiled and bent over to kiss my collarbone, and sniffing my neck like a cute little rabbit. I giggled. "So do you and even sweeter."

"Okay enough. People will think you're into some real kinky shit if you keep sniffing my neck," I laughed.

He engulfed me in his arms and began sniffing my neck again. "Who gives a damn? Your skin is so soft and you outrageously desirable."

"Save if for the bed, Drake."

"Mmm, don't mind if I do." He joked.

I smiled and grabbed my bag, "Could we please go now?"

"Yup."

We went hand in hand out of the hospital and into his truck. My skin was almost transparent due to the lack of vitamin D, and the sun felt good on my veneer skin. "Mmm. I missed the sun so much."

He turned on the motor and pointed at my arms and legs, "Looked like your skin missed it too."

I hit him playfully and let my head roll across the seat. "Maybe we can go to some private beach or something for our honeymoon, don't you think?"

"Well shit, I already bought tickets for Greenland."

I glared at him. He laughed and blew me an immature kiss. "I'm kidding; no need to go into death mode."

"So where are we going?"

He tapped his chin while we waited for the light to turn green. "Where do you want to go?"

"Ooh!!" I screamed out, "Let's go to San Torini!"

His eyebrows fell, "Where the hell is that?"

"Oh you know. It's in Greece. My mom and I visited there when I was a younger. It was so romantic, but of course I didn't have a friend to really enjoy it with. My mom certainly had plenty."

He chuckled, "Alright then."

I turned on the radio and tapped my fingers on my knees to the beat of the group Sleek and Sultry's "I am Hot". Out of the blue Drake asked me something I was prepared for. "So are you ready for tomorrow." And by that he meant our wedding.

I didn't look him in the eyes for a few seconds; I just stared through the window watching the trees that blurred by. I was beyond ready for tomorrow. We've only known each other for two months, but we love each other like any other couple with a few years together or maybe even more. After my coma, I now know how well Drake and I care for each other. We just do even with our differences. I love him so much, and he loves me back. We're two sculptures made from the same clay. I smiled broadly and said, "The better question is... Drake, are you."